MAVERICKS:
FIVE AGAINST THE LAW

LONGRIDERS OF THE WEST ™

MAVERICKS

LANCE CLAYTON•DOC GRIMSON•CHARLIE PARR•LOCKJAW JOHNSON•FLINT MADDOX

FIVE AGAINST
THE LAW

By Kent Thorn

POPULAR PUBLICATIONS • 2018

PUBLISHING HISTORY

"Five Against the Law" originally appeared in the September 1934 issue of *Mavericks* magazine (Vol. 1, No. 1). Copyright 1934, 1961 by Popular Publications, Inc. All Rights Reserved.

CHAPTER 1
BRAND OF WANTED MEN

L ESSER MEN might have looked grim. Riding in to sell a herd of wet cattle to Ogalally Pete's outfit was scarcely the kind of amusement which most people would have chosen for a warm spring morning, particularly when outnumbered several to one. Yet this five rode with the casual good humor of men on an outing.

"'You're a dee-stang-ay ornament to the culinary art,' says the tenderfoot." Doc Grimson was talking, his fine gray eyes alive with humor. "Right out like that! 'You're a dee-stang-ay ornament to the culinary art.' Well, Ma Rumsay kind of flushes up. I can see she figures it for a compliment all right, but not savvying the French language she doesn't know what to do with it. Lockjaw, however, is suffering under no such handicap. He knows it's an insult and that's all there is to it. Before Ma can get out a word he jumps to his feet and goes for his six-gun. 'Stranger,' he yells, 'take that back!'"

Charlie Parr shook with sudden internal laughter, but all that escaped from under his flowing white mustache was a chuckle. Despite the age of the mustache which veiled it, it was a curiously young and musical chuckle, just as the keen, unfaded blue eyes beneath the bushy white brows were extraordinarily young and sparkling. He turned and glanced back over the dusty backs of the herd to where the habitually silent Lockjaw

Johnson rode swing, as though to assure himself of the actual existence of that man whose almost superhuman dumbness had been the delight and the curse of his life for so many years.

Across from Lockjaw rode Lance Clayton, singing:

> "So I'll sell my outfit as fast as I can,
> And I won't punch cows for no damn man."

His voice came clear and young and joyous through the crystalline morning air. Behind the herd, almost obscured by dust, was Flint Maddox. Flint, Charlie reflected, rode drag by preference. He was so crazy about cattle he even got some satisfaction out of eating their dust on the rare occasions when the crowd had anything to do with the critters.

2

"The Easterner was naturally taken a-back," Doc Grimson went on with relish. "'Why—why,' says he, stammering, 'I didn't say anything.' 'You said plenty,' Lockjaw tells him, waving the six-gun under his nose. 'You can't insult no ladies around here!'"

A man with a rifle stepped out onto the trail ahead of them. "Hold 'em here," he called out, "and come into camp to see the chief."

Two riders spurred out from behind some rocks, evidently to take over the herd.

Doc Grimson and Charlie Parr exchanged a glance of amusement. "Thought so," Charlie grunted.

"Got a little reception all arranged for us, with all his boys around him," Doc observed drily. "There ain't more than twelve or fifteen, but every one of 'em as poison as a hydrophobia skunk. Have to be, to ride with a murderin' dry-gulcher like Ogalally." Doc turned and waved to the others to come on.

Ogalally Pete was a big curly-headed man with beady black eyes and the grin of a hyena; the swashbuckling type of outlaw leader. Silk shirt, a band of Mexican wheel-work on his sombrero, silver buttoned bolero, and fancy, hand-worked cartridge belts. By reputation he had the blood-thirsty ferocity of a lobo out for the kill.

Charlie Parr eyed Ogalally Pete with new contempt. Charlie could stand neither a man who killed unnecessarily nor a liar, and Ogalally Pete was a fine example of both—with other things thrown in. He let a casual glance run over Ogalally's followers. They stood, a round dozen of them, in a semi-circle behind their leader, and it didn't need anybody as acute as Charlie Parr to realize that they were waiting for trouble. The exaggerated carelessness of their attitudes advertised that as clearly as did the fact that they stood clear of one another, gun-hands free.

"Nice-lookin' herd yo're givin' us," said Ogalally, jovially. His thumbs were hooked in his fancy crossed cartridge belts and he looked like a man enjoying a private joke.

"Givin' is right," observed Doc Grimson drily, "considerin' the price we're getting for them. And by the way, we'll have that now—ten thousand dollars."

Ogalally Pete threw back his head and laughed, but his eyes were wary. "You didn't take that serious about bein' paid?" he asked.

DOC GRIMSON wasn't standing in the gunman's posture, and nobody saw his hands move. Nobody realized that they had moved until his two Colts were trained directly and unwaveringly on Ogalally Pete's stomach. Then one of the outlaw's followers belatedly and foolishly started his draw. He stopped it before the gun had cleared leather. One of Charley Parr's ancient weapons, its barrel as menacing as a cannon's, was trained on the middle button of the man's vest. Charlie was a shade slower on the draw than Doc Grimson. But it wasn't a shade that would have proved any manner of benefit to the average gunman.

"You'd better take it quite seriously, my friend," Doc said quietly to Ogalally Pete.

The outlaw's features flashed a mixture of astonishment, chagrin and fear. But after a second he found his tongue. "Hey now," he said, with an attempt at his previous joviality. "You

5

don't want to get hairy over a little joke, Doc. Why, you ought to know I wouldn't try no ranny over fellers like you."

"Sure," said Doc, grinning. "I like a joke as well as the next man. We'll all have a good laugh over this one—when the money is paid."

Better men than Ogalally Pete had tried to bluff this five, with just as little success. Different as they were, they had two qualities in common—fearlessness and loyalty. As a team they made a formidable combination. And men from the northern-most ranges of Montana to the alkali-flats of the Rio had learned to respect and fear that combination; hard-riding hombres of the hoot-owl trail as well as law-abiding ranchers and townsmen took care not to cross them. For a dozen reasons, the chief of which was pride, this quintet lived outside the law, but the law they made for themselves was sometimes surprising and dis-concerting to other riders of the long trail.

Of the five, Doc Grimson was the mystery. Not even his partners knew just why he had come West or what had happened in the life of this slender, quiet, courteous man, whose supple skillful fingers seemed to be able to render life and deal death with equal facility, to drive him out from society into the hard, dangerous world of wanted men. They had rare glimpses of a cultivated, brilliant mind which was not hidden by the range lingo he affected, and they knew him for a surgeon of extraor-dinary skill.

But if Doc Grimson remembered another life than that which he now led, he gave no sign of regretting it. He had made himself into a cutting instrument, hard and sharp as a lancet.

He said little, watched men and events with a cool, humorous gray eye, and drank danger as a connoisseur savors rare old whisky.

EVEN CHARLIE PARR recognized in him a natural leader, and Charlie had spent a long life devoted chiefly to not knuckling under to any man. Trapper, buffalo hunter, and prospector, had been a government scout until a certain brash Major Andrews had attempted to give him foolish orders, and had threatened to withhold his pay for disobedience. Charlie had led the detachment safely back to the fort and then had departed. Mysteriously, half a hundred prime army mules chose that occasion also to take a *pasear* from which they never returned. After that Charlie had joined up with Boot Hill Kennedy, until that famous outlaw's carelessness about killing people caused an argument between the two—an argument which resulted fatally to Kennedy.

Thereafter Charlie led the bunch, until a bank president's young wife surprised them in the act of robbing the bank. She put herself before the safe and declared they would have to kill her before they ruined her husband. It would have been easy to overpower her, but Charlie forbade anyone to lay a hand on her and called the robbery off. The gang expressed the opinion that this was carrying gallantry too far, and got itself a new leader. All except Lockjaw, who wouldn't have known how to go about changing a loyalty even if he had wanted to.

Accident had brought the pair finally across the trail of Flint Maddox—a desperate and embittered man. Flint, still under thirty-five, had had about all the bad luck one man could have.

7

A range-hog, with the help of the law, had driven him broke on his small spread, and during Flint's absence in town, his wife died in an unsuccessful attempt to rescue their two small children from a fire of evidently incendiary origin. Flint had no proof that his neighbor enemy was guilty of setting the fire, but he had a considerable moral certainty of it. He killed the range-hog and his foreman in a saloon fight and then took the trail with a crooked sheriff some jumps behind him.

Then Lance Clayton had turned up. Woman trouble had made difficulties between Lance and the law. A lady in distress had appealed to him for money he didn't have. The case seemed to be urgent so Lance went out and stuck up the local gambling house, was recognized and left town in a hurry after turning the proceeds over to the lady, who did not refuse them but who lately on moral grounds, repudiated the donor both publicly and privately. Lance felt considerably disillusioned, but nothing could damage his irrepressible good spirits for long and, once outside the law, he was made to order for this gang. He stood six feet one without his boots; packed a pair of hips as slender as a girl's waist and a pair of shoulders with the spread of a barn door; was a top hand with cattle; could sit anything with four legs and had a gun-hand second only to Doc and Charlie. Under their tuition, in fact, he was threatening to surpass them.

THAT WAS the five which stood face to face with Ogalally Pete's killers. In the silence which followed Doc Grimson's last retort, Doc holstered his guns. The others did likewise. It was a gesture of contempt which had its effect. Ogalally's crowd looked disconcerted and a little apprehensive. It was plain that none of them wanted a fight and that each was a little afraid somebody might get up the nerve to start one. It was a tight situation, with plenty of dynamite in it. One wrong move from anybody, and the place would be a shambles within five seconds.

Charlie Parr grinned at the man who had tried to draw. "We're always ready for fun an' games," he observed.

"Yeah," agreed Lance Clayton, his eyes dancing. "But don't forget there are flies on you, fella. There's a big blue-bottomed one a-settin' on your shoulder now. One of us might get the notion to shoot them flies off you."

Bam! A six-gun bellowed like the voice of doom. Involuntarily, startled hands raced for holstered Colts.

Doc Grimson's voice cracked warningly. "Hold it!" His guns had come out again like blue streaks, the worn shiny barrels of Charlie Parr's old-fashioned hoglegs an infinitesimal part of a second behind them. Again that lightning draw bettered the speed of the men before them by a narrow but entirely sufficient margin. Charlie Parr turned to where Lockjaw Johnson stood, a thin trickle of smoke still oozing from the barrel of his Colt.

"What in thunder are you tryin' to do, you dad-blasted jawhead?" he stormed. "Dad-blame my socks if I ain't a mind to git some dynamite and blast into that there head of yourn until I find out what you got in there in place of brains. You tryin' to start a massacre, you hammer-headed hopper-grass?"

Lockjaw looked injured. "I wasn't doin' nothin' but shoot that there fly off him," he said sulkily. "Lance said for to shoot the flies off'n him, didn't yuh, Lance?" He turned appealingly toward Lance, but that young man was in no condition to answer questions. He was doubled over and pounding himself violently on the thighs. Curious, choked sounds came out of him. After a little, however, he straightened up and came over to Lockjaw. "Some shot," he gurgled. "Some shot, Lockjaw." The hysterical tears streamed down his face. "You shore got that fly, boy—no foolin'!"

The man who had had the fly on his shoulder flushed angrily but said nothing. From time to time he looked wonderingly at the shoulder where the unfortunate insect had perched. He had felt the wind of the bullet through the cloth and there remained a fleck of blood in which was stuck the leg of a fly.

Charlie Parr raised resigned eyes to heaven. Doc Grimson straightened his face with difficulty and then turned on Ogalally Pete an eye in which amusement and menace were mixed. "Now I reckon we'll have that money," he said.

The outlaw leader delayed no longer. He reached in his pocket and pulled out a heavy sheaf of banknotes. He didn't say anything, because there was nothing to say.

That was the moment for Doc and the rest of them to leave. They could have ridden off then, safe. But their luck didn't want it that way. As they turned toward their horses, one of the two riders who had ridden out to take charge of the herd, galloped into camp and dismounted before Ogalally Pete. He was an extremely young, good-looking boy, and at the moment he was white-faced with excitement. "Those are Flyin' Bar M critters," he flung at Ogalally tensely. "Every one of 'em!"

The outlaw stared, then threw back his head and bellowed with laughter. "By gravy," he got out, "that's a good one." The youngster evidently didn't share his amusement. His face colored and he turned angrily on Doc Grimson. "Where'd you rustle those cows, you?" he demanded fiercely.

Doc Grimson eyed him speculatively a moment and then evidently decided to answer. "Why," he drawled. "We picked 'em up over the Border a ways. What's it to you?"

"What's it to me, you dirty rustler?" the boy snarled, his hand going to his gun. "They're my cattle—that's what it is to me."

Doc Grimson betrayed consciousness of the insult only by a slightly raised eyebrow. "I'm guessin' you're wrong," he said quietly. "They were Mexican cattle when we persuaded them to emigrate, and right now they wear Ogalally's brand, he having paid for them."

The boy whirled on the outlaw. "You can't do this, Ogalally," he snapped. "You can't buy my father's cattle from this rustler."

Ogalally stopped grinning and his eyes grew cruel. "What in hell are you talkin' about?" he rumbled brutally. "I buy cattle or take cattle where I like and when I like. You ain't a little boy workin' on your dad's spread any more. Them cows belong to this gang now. You get your split on the profits, same as the rest—if you're good. Now git back an' ride herd like I told you."

CHAPTER 2
THE KID FILLS HIS HAND

THE BOY'S face went white again. It was evident that the full consciousness of his position had just begun to dawn on him. His eyes went from the contemptuous cruelty

11

in Ogalally's gaze to the hard, sneering faces of the men around him. After a moment he relaxed and his face went expressionless.

"I reckon I forgot," he said slowly. "I reckon I must sound kind of green and foolish talkin' about rustlers an' so on." He forced a smile. "Seein' the old familiar faces of them critters kind of got me excited, so I spoke out of turn. I forgot I wasn't on that side of the fence any longer."

He turned to get on his horse.

Doc Grimson smiled faintly to himself. The kid had done his best to cover up a bad mistake, he decided, but he didn't believe the sudden change of front had fooled anybody, and when Ogalally Pete spoke again it was to confirm this opinion.

"Never mind about riding out again, Hewitt," the outlaw said suavely. "I reckon it ain't right to make you ride herd on your old man's cows. Jake'll take your place. You stay here."

Young Hewitt hesitated. You could see his instinct made him want to go back to the cattle, but it was better policy not to make a point of it. He dismounted again in silence.

Doc Grimson exchanged a glance with Charlie Parr. The latter shrugged slightly. Neither of them would have given a plugged nickel for Hewitt's chances of getting through the night alive. Charlie's shrug meant simply that it wasn't any of their business. After all, Doc reflected, it would not be exactly to their advantage either if the kid got away to report and make trouble. But his gray eyes clouded a little with reluctance as he decided that Charlie was right. There wasn't anything they could do.

Flint Maddox spoke up then in his easy, soft-voiced drawl. "That kid's plenty green," he observed. "Didn't know you had 'em like that, Ogalally. If I thought the rest of your gang was like him I'd shore like to start a poker game around here."

Ogalally's face lighted up. Doc Grimson guessed that Ogalally saw in this a way to get his money back. "Poker!" he exclaimed. "Now you're talkin' our language. We'd shore admire to set in a little friendly game. What do you say, boys?"

"Count me in as number one," Flint told him.

Doc groaned within himself. He saw what was coming. Flint rarely played poker; cared nothing for it. If he was letting himself into this game, it could be only for one reason: he didn't want to leave. The cowman in him wanted to stick by this kid who had lost his cattle and gotten himself into a jam by talking too much.

"Now that's plumb surprisin'," said Lance Clayton blithely. "You fellas are talkin' just what I been thinkin'. I'm fair honin' to set in on a little poker."

Doc saw Charlie Parr frown and start to speak. Before he could do so Lockjaw emerged from the silence long enough to say "Me too!" with enthusiasm. Charlie Parr looked at him in weary disgust. It was a sort of unwritten law among the five that in ordinary matters a majority vote ruled, though they all looked to Charlie and Doc, but especially Doc, for leadership in whatever they undertook. Lance Clayton, Doc knew, must realize Flint's purpose as well as anyone, but Lockjaw, it was equally certain, was oblivious to it. He had spoken up because he wanted to play poker—a game at which he invariably lost—

13

and for no other reason. Doc grinned. Dumbness, as so often in legislative bodies, had cast the deciding vote.

When young Hewitt came back from picketing his horse, Ogalally Pete herded him with genial and sinister insistence into the poker game. The youngster accepted with an assumption of cheerful good-fellowship, but he looked nervous. His face under its coating of tan was bloodless and his eyes were those of an animal seeking a way out of a trap. He had lost his head at the sight of his father's cattle but he was no fool. Another sort of leader might have taken a chance on keeping him close until the herd was disposed of, but not Ogalally Pete. He would take the simple way. His distrust once aroused, he would kill.

And that which Bill Hewitt knew was also known by every other man there, with the possible exception of Lockjaw. The camp took on the atmosphere of a jail on the morning of an execution. Men moved and spoke with elaborate carelessness but their movements and their speech gave the effect of being calculated, careful and subdued. Worst of all, they avoided Hewitt's gaze. When he caught them looking at him, they glanced away, but in the instant of the shift he could read the knowledge of his finish in their eyes. A glint of mockery, of ferocity, of contemptuous pity—it took different forms but the meaning was the same. Death sat there in the bright noon light like a shadowy presence, tangible, inescapable....

DOC GRIMSON and Charlie Parr watched the game from a little distance, backs strategically placed against some protecting rocks. Charlie Parr's expression was sour.

Doc said speculatively, "I kind of hate to see it."

"Now don't you go gittin' soft on me," Charlie broke out irascibly. "Have some sense! They ain't goin' to let that jasper get away, an' there ain't nothin' sensible we can do about it."

Doc said nothing. He knew Charlie was right. Charlie was a practical man. He had a merciful lack of imagination, and he had looked on sudden death too often to be much impressed by it. But this was different. Doc wondered how in the world a kid like that had ever gotten into this gang. He hadn't been bred to the long trail and there must be suddenly something horrible to him in the thought of dying this way, stupidly, on the wrong side of the fence.

"Here it goes," said Charlie suddenly, hooking his thumbs in his belt.

"I saw you palm that ace, you crooked skunk!" It was the fly-shouldered gun-slinger who rasped that, coming to his feet in one swift movement.

Young Bill Hewitt got to his feet more slowly. His face was drained of color but his eyes were steady and there was a curious expression of relief on his features. The shot wasn't to come from behind, at least.

His voice came stiffly through dry lips but it was calm and clear. "Yo're a liar," he said simply.

Doc could see the thoughts racing back of Flint's forehead. He hadn't any excuse to interfere. This was legitimate, on the surface. If he horned in, he'd be in the wrong and he'd take his partners with him into a bad fight. And Doc knew, as he'd known all along, that Flint wouldn't do that.

"Fill yore hand!" the gunman snapped.

The boy before him didn't hesitate. His hand flashed to the butt of his holstered Colt, but though the draw wouldn't have looked slow to ordinary eyes it was slow—slow as molasses to Doc's critical eye. The heavy six-gun was just clearing leather when the gunman's first shot blasted into the midday silence. The slug nearly knocked the kid off his feet. He stumbled backward and sat down suddenly, and the gunman's second shot nearly missed him—ripped along his neck by the shoulder muscle. Doc Grimson could see the blood spurt. But the first shot would be enough, he guessed. It had smashed square through the chest.

The gunman had only fired those two shots, but now he appeared suddenly to doubt whether they had done their work or not. Deliberately he raised his gun and leveled again.

Lance Clayton moved then, cursing. He drew and laid the barrel of his heavy Colt across the gunman's forearm in one lightning motion. The gunman dropped his weapon and roared a curse of pain.

"What are you tryin' to pull—murder?" Lance snarled.

"Steady—steady!" Doc Grimson called in a patient voice.

Ogalally Pete's face was dark, but if he was angry, his mind appeared to be working clearly enough. That first shot had probably done his business; what had happened afterward wasn't worth a general slaughter. He quieted his men with a word.

Doc Grimson knelt beside Hewitt. Lance Clayton followed him. Flint would have done likewise except that Charlie Parr's commanding eye picked up and held him back with Lockjaw.

For all five of them to group themselves with their backs un-protected would simply invite murder.

AFTER A brief examination Doc shook his head soberly. The bullet had smashed a rib in front, torn through the lung, just missing the heart, and lodged, probably against a rib in the back. He got up and went to his horse. He always carried in-struments in his saddlebags.

Young Hewitt looked at Lance Clayton. "It's no use," he said faintly. "I'm done for."

"Maybe not," Lance said simply. "You don't know the doc. He's a sawbones what knows his business, even if he don't follow it."

"I don't know why you sat in on this play," the boy gasped out, "but I'm shore obliged to you. Listen, would you do some-thing for me?"

"I reckon."

"In my vest pocket you'll find a wallet. It's got nearly a thousand dollars in it—my cut of a—stage job we—pulled." It was plain he was getting weaker. "I can't trust—any of the—gang. Will you take it to my old man—it's the Flying M Bar spread near Longhorn. Know it?"

"I know about where Longhorn is."

"Don't tell dad where—the money came from. It's not enough but—it might help—some."

Lance reached out and took the wallet. When he opened it to count the money a girl's face looked out at him from a faded photograph. It was a saucy, pretty face, delicately carved, with big dark eyes which looked at once tender and gay. Staring at it and conscious of its fascination Lance tried to remind himself that he was disgusted with women. Silly creatures. They only got in a man's way and then let him down in a pinch for somebody else. Nevertheless, his voice sounded a little brusque as he said to Hewitt, "I'd think if you had a girl like that you'd have kept out of this business."

"It's my—sister," the boy told him. "I joined up with Ogalally because dad was—broke. Somebody's after dad—we don't—know who. He—loses cattle. I think it's Ed Lowery. Claire—sister—doesn't believe it. Don't tell her I—was in this."

Doc Grimson came back, with his instruments and a bottle of whisky. He poured whisky in the wound and got out a probe which he had previously sterilized by holding it in the flame of the fire and then pouring whisky on it. It was a rough and ready method which once would have filled the doctor himself with horror, but which no longer did. He had learned, he said, that there were "plenty of fancy trimmings that good surgery can get along without."

"Have to probe for the bullet," he told Hewitt briefly. "Sorry I can't give you any whisky to drink. Don't want to stimulate your heart while you're still losing blood. Hang on—it'll hurt."

It did. The cold sweat of agony sprang out on the boy's forehead, but he set his jaw and held still until finally he lost consciousness from pain and loss of blood.

"Any chance?" Lance asked when the boy's wounds had been thoroughly bandaged.

"Probably none," Doc Grimson replied crisply. "The only

thing that might give him a chance in a hundred is that he's young."

"What about moving him?"

"He'd die. And the chance isn't worth it to stay with him."

Lance nodded reluctantly. "Come on then," he said. "Let's get goin'. We've got some business ahead."

"What do you mean?"

"Tell you later."

"Son, don't you ever get tired of trouble?"

Lance grinned in sudden delight. "You crazy son of a gun," he said affectionately. "If we ever got out of trouble you'd die of boredom!"

CHAPTER 3
LOCKJAW MAKES A KILL

THEY HAD ridden a mile south, toward the distant gap which formed the first gate to Ogalally Pete's stronghold, before Lance finished the story of what Bill Hewitt had told him.

"It smells skunk around the Flying M Bar," he ended. "And seein' that I've got to deliver the money, what do you say we sit in on the game down there. I'm figgerin' we can clean things up an' maybe do ourselves some good at the same time."

There was a long silence, during which Lance rode with his serenity unruffled. He was accustomed to the deliberate processes of his partners' minds, when there was no occasion which demanded immediate action.

19

The silence was broken finally by Lockjaw. "Shore!" said he, with the pleased expression of one upon whom complete comprehension has suddenly dawned. "If this Bar M ranny is that soft, it's a regular set-up. Once we git in with him we can take everything that ain't nailed down."

The others stared. None of the four had ever really gotten used to Lockjaw's mental processes.

"That wasn't exactly what I meant, Lockjaw," Lance said seriously. "You see; I was aimin' to help this Bar M ranny—not rob him. You see, since we've agreed to take his money to him, why—er—" he paused. It was always pretty difficult to present fine points of morals so that Lockjaw could take them in.

Lockjaw looked bewildered, but he was accustomed to finding himself in the wrong. He merely said uncomfortably, "Shore, Lance—anyway you say—if it's all right with the rest of 'em." He looked for confirmation to Charlie Parr. But Charlie said, irascibly: "No sense in it whatever. This here Bar M crowd ain't nothin' to us. I'm agin it!"

Flint Maddox said: "The way I see it, we're to blame for gettin' that young feller killed. If we hadn't rustled his cattle and drove 'em up here, he'd have been all right. It's up to us to do what we can about it."

Lance glanced at him affectionately. He had been pretty sure of Flint's support. When it came to helping anyone out, Flint was always in favor of it. You'd think the tragedy that had wrecked his life would have made him bitter. It had left its mark, all right, but it was a mark only of sadness. The man's big, homely features were set in a permanent mask of melancholy.

He never laughed and rarely smiled, which fooled some people into thinking him hard, maybe because he was a hard-handed man when it came to action—tough and able. But when he did smile, there was a rare sort of sweetness in it, and you could guess then that when it came to certain things the man's heart was soft as butter.

Charlie Parr said irritably: "Hell! We didn't have any way to know they was his cows. We come into new country, drift down to the Border, pick out old Bautista's ranch to do a little wide-loopin' on, make us a deal to sell the critters to Ogalally, an' then we're to blame because a kid gets antes in his shirts an' contracts lead poisonin'. Me, I don't claim to know all the brands in these parts. Besides, how was we to figger this Mex hadn't bought the cattle legitimate. We had enough trouble gittin' 'em—didn't we?—what with havin' to shoot up a couple of them chili cow-nurses of his."

Lance grinned and said nothing. Charlie had to be against any idea of taking any trouble for anybody else. At least, he had to talk that way. If you turned around and agreed with him it'd make him madder'n a preacher in a cactus bed.

Doc Grimson looked grave. "I guess the boys are right, Charlie," he said. "We didn't mean the young fellow any harm but we did him plenty just the same. It looks as though it was up to us to lend a hand and help out his folks—since he's out of it."

Charlie tried to appear disgruntled. "All right," he said disgustedly. "Let's ride." He added sardonically: "I reckon you figger to turn the money we got from Ogalally over to him.

21

Well, that'll be better than gittin' into a cattle war where we'd only collect a lot of bullets, anyway."

"The money we got from Ogalally wouldn't make up half the value of that herd," Lance pointed out. "If the old man's gettin' the steel throwed into him by his skunk neighbor he'll likely need more than that. We ought to be willin' to set in on the game down there, just the same."

DOC WAS silent a moment, then his eyes began to twinkle. "That's right," he agreed thoughtfully. "If we had the herd back now…" he began and then stopped.

Lance stared. He let out a sudden whoop. "Buckin' tarantulas, Doc! You don't mean to…?"

Doc Grimson looked solemn. "This Ogalally Pete is a sinful hombre," he said. "Do you think it would be right to leave a lot of poor dumb helpless critters in hands like his?"

Flint Maddox's melancholy disappeared. He grinned. Even Charlie Parr couldn't suppress a smile of sudden pleasure. It was a lovely idea. "Hell!" he said slowly, "why not? There ain't but about fifteen of 'em."

Lance leaned over and clapped the uncomprehending Lockjaw on the shoulder. "We're goin' back and rustle them cattle from Ogalally Pete, fella," he explained exuberantly. "Get it?"

Lockjaw's face glowed. It was plain' that he had not been listening to the talk but that he thought this an inspiration. "Shore!" he said. "Then we can take 'em into Mexico and sell 'em again!"

Charlie Parr chuckled. "Lockjaw's right at that," he said.

"That'd be the sensible thing to do. But you an' me, Lockjaw, has throwed in with a crowd of locoed buckaroos what don't know a silver dollar from a plugged nickel. We're gonna start a riot with fifteen men just for the fun of driving them consarned critters back to this Flying M Bar spread—wherever that is! Spill your plan, Doc."

"It's simple," Doc said. "The way I see it, Ogalally won't drive those cattle this afternoon. There's grass and water in that valley there and the herd's gaunted by the drive from Mexico. He'll let 'em rest this afternoon and tonight. Tomorrow he'll start 'em up toward his main camp and hold 'em somewhere up there until he gets a buyer for 'em. So we've got plenty of time. We'll ride on a ways—it's not more than an hour's slow ride to the gap there, where we'll be out of sight. Then we'll work back under cover and hit the cattle just after sunset when it's still light."

"Wouldn't it be better to wait until dark?" Flint asked.

"No," Doc shook his head. "We couldn't protect our rear that way. Ogalally's got too many men. In the dark they'd be all over us. This way we can shove the cattle down to the gap before dark, and once in that deep canyon two men can hold off an army."

"What'll we do—stampede the herd and make a running fight of it?" Lance asked.

"Not if we can help it. You and Flint and Lockjaw will get up in the woods and brush on the west of the valley and do something to decoy the fellows who are riding herd over to where you can take 'em without any fight. Charlie and I will work up on the other side of the valley and be handy to keep the gang off you in case anything goes wrong."

By sunset the three who were to drive the cattle were in position. They had moved slowly and carefully most of the afternoon and were satisfied that they had gotten into the woods without being seen by any of Ogalally's lookouts. They left their mounts picketed back in the brush and crawled stealthily up toward the edge.

The cattle, they knew, were pretty well spread out over the narrow valley, which made a natural holding ground, and Flint and Lance had agreed that they would rope the calf of a wet cow from the edge of the bushes, and encourage it to set up a racket which would bring one or both of the riders over. Probably only one would come and if he were taken silently the other would eventually drift over to see what had happened to him.

THEY MOVED slowly, making no noise and scarcely stirring a bush. All three were accomplished hunters, but of them all Lockjaw's progress was most silent. He had had the advantage of Charlie Parr's training, and he moved with the swift, silent sureness of an Indian. Lance, on his right, watched him with admiration. Lockjaw had his qualities, all right, he thought. Mostly you could count on him to be dumb with an ingenious and talented dumbness like nobody else's in the world. But give him a simple, practical job to do, where he knew exactly what was expected of him, and there wasn't a better man on earth. He was a good hand with cattle, an accomplished woodsman, and, though his draw was slow as molasses, he was one of the best shots with either rifle or six-gun, in the gang. And that was saying a lot!

It was at about that point in his reflections that they saw the mountain lion. The big cat had been stalking the cattle and, intent on his prey, was unaware of their approach. They nearly stumbled on him at the moment when he had left cover and was creeping, belly-down—a magnificent tawny, deadly sight—toward a group of recently weaned calves.

Instantly, Lance and Flint realized their luck. One of the herd-riders, they could see through the fringe of bushes, was not more than two hundred yards away. His attention would surely be attracted by the frightened calves, once the mountain lion had made his spring. The cat would lose his meal, but the enemy would be delivered into their hands. Lance decided that the rider would shout to his companion and that both would probably come into the bushes on the trail of the marauding cat. They could take them both without noise or trouble. It was a heaven-sent chance.

And then Lockjaw Johnson shot the lion.

Lance and Flint stood transfixed by a kind of superhuman amazement. The thing had happened—was happening. Their senses attested it. But it was entirely too improbable to believe.

"Got him!" Lockjaw whispered excitedly, and went jumping out through the bushes toward his prey.

They saw the nearby rider look up, startled. Then he evidently saw Lockjaw come out into the open and he put his horse into a gallop to investigate. Lockjaw, apparently, had forgotten his very existence. His instincts as a cattleman had crowded out even the memory of why he was there! He stood over the dying cat, and, as though he owned all the time in the world, reloaded his gun.

The rider pulled up suddenly, and the Colt in his hand spoke twice. Lockjaw's hat leapt from his head. Lance and Flint fired, but the range for them was longer and although one of the bullets creased him, the gunman kept his saddle. Then Lockjaw's gun bellowed—just once.

The rider flung one arm wide and leaned forward in the saddle like a man making a stately bow. Then he fell sideways and forward to the ground and nobody who saw him fall could have doubted that he would never move again.

The rider on the other side of the valley had started toward the disturbance, but seeing his partner fall from the saddle, he set off at a dead run for camp. Lance cursed in a low, steady voice for a moment, then grinned at Flint, who grinned back. "That does it!" Lance said. "What do you say, Flint—want to take a chance? They'll be on our necks in two minutes."

"Hell," Flint grinned. "There's only fourteen of 'em left."

"Get to the horses then, quick! Well have to stampede 'em. Lockjaw!"

Lockjaw came toward them. He looked faintly worried.

"Say, Lance," he said, doubtfully. "I reckon I oughtn't to have shot that there varmint."

CHAPTER 4
STAMPEDE

L ANCE HAD no time for the ironic comments which sprang to his lips. He merely said: "Come on!" and set off on a run to the horses.

Twenty seconds later they came charging through the trees and brush at a break-neck pace and raced up the valley to get behind the herd. Once there, they fanned out, working like a well-oiled machine, and came at the grazing cows whooping and firing over their heads.

Slowly, like a wave rolling in on itself, the herd got under way, gathered speed, was off in a thunder of hoofs and a great bellowing and snorting of fright. Once the stampede was started, Flint and Lockjaw raced for the flanks, to prevent a split-off, while Lance kept to the rear, glancing over his shoulder in momentary expectation of the aroused outlaws.

Lance was under no illusions as to the kind of scrap they would be in for, but on the other hand the idea that they were committing suicide never once occurred to him. Doc Grimson and Charlie Parr would sit in on the party and while five against fourteen was long odds, Lance knew by experience that straight shooting could make up for a lot of numbers. His guess was that Ogalally Pete and his crowd would come fanning out into the open, spraying lead all over the landscape. That was what men usually did in a hot running fight. Whereas Doc and Charlie and Flint and Lockjaw would be handling their Winchesters with the slow, cool certainty of men at target practice.

27

It probably wouldn't take long to whittle Ogalally's gang down to their size.

But seconds and then minutes went by without any sight of the outlaws. Not a sound, not a movement came from the small mesa above the valley rim which harbored the camp. Lance began to worry. This wasn't included in his calculations. He scanned the side hills anxiously, wondering if Ogalally had cut them off by getting to the gap ahead of them. There in that deep canyon the five could be ambushed and cut down to a man. They might never have a chance to shoot at all.

But the straight trail to the gap was that which the stampede was taking, and the valley widened below. Lance didn't see how horsemen could follow the rough country along the hills and get into the gap without being seen, even after the cattle had run themselves out and begun their first mad charge.

Still the minutes passed without offering an answer to his questions. The tired cattle slowed, came to a walk, took up a pace which seemed to Lance not faster than the crawl of worms. Ahead the canyon entrance loomed clearer and clearer. Behind, the landscape showed bare, deserted, peaceful in the clear late-afternoon light.

Where the devil were Doc and Charlie, Lance asked himself worriedly. Had anything happened to them? Had Ogalally trapped them and then taken a hidden trail through the hills that would bring him out into the deep canyon? Lance could remember no opening in those steep, towering walls. The whole thing seemed impossible, inexplicable. He shouted to Flint, who rode back to join him.

"This is a funny one," Lance said as the other rode up.

Flint, too, looked worried. "Yeah," he said soberly. "I can't quite make it out. What you reckon happened to Doc and Charlie?"

"If it was anybody but them," Lance said, "I'd know what happened to 'em. But it just ain't in the cards that those two would let themselves be topped off like that, without even a shot bein' fired. It just don't make sense."

"You reckon we ought to ride back and see, Lance?"

"*We* can't. It'll have to be me. You and Lockjaw can handle the cows all right. Hold 'em right at the mouth of the canyon—hear? Don't try to go through without me. I'll be back as soon as I can make it."

Lockjaw rode up. When he heard Lance's plan he looked stubborn. "One man can hold 'em here," he said. "I'm goin' with you, Lance."

"Say, listen," Flint cut in. "These critters are too tired to go anywhere tonight. We'll all three go."

Lance shook his head. "No," he said. "If those skunks have got back into the canyon by some secret way, we need somebody here to—"

"They ain't got back into the canyon," Lockjaw interrupted positively. "I know, because—"

"You can't tell, Lockjaw."

"I'm shore of it, because—"

"Listen, fella—it looks impossible all right. But I tell you we got to count on it."

"Well," said Lockjaw doubtfully, "mebbe yo're right, Lance.

I just thought that maybe that there dust-cloud there behind Doc and Charlie...."

LANCE WHIRLED and swore. He had been sitting with his back to the trail. Now, far off down the valley floor, he could make out two tiny figures, riding fast; and far behind them, almost invisible in the rapidly fading light, was a dust cloud that must have been made by at least a dozen more men.

Lance looked at Lockjaw wonderingly and shook his head. "Some man, this Lockjaw," he said. "Don't nothin' get by him— not even cougars."

By the time Doc and Charlie rode up they had gotten the cattle started down the canyon.

"What happened to Ogalally Pete?" Lance demanded grinning.

"He got delayed a little," Doc told him gravely. "We're expecting him to join us pretty soon."

"You boys have a nice time a-poppin' off yore guns?" asked Charlie Parr politely.

"Why you see," Flint explained. "Lockjaw took a notion to go cougar hunting."

"It was just somethin' that kind of come over him," Lance put in.

Lockjaw looked embarrassed. "He was goin' to kill a calf, Charlie," he defended himself worriedly.

"So we had to stampede 'em and kill twenty calves," said Lance. "Where were you when the party started?"

"We were having our siesta back of some nice shady rocks,"

Doc told him. "And just by accident the rocks were right above Ogalally's camp. Maybe you noticed them this morning."

"So when a rider come in full of sweat and astonishment," Charlie went on, "we told Ogalally that you gents had changed your minds about sellin' him the cattle."

Lance grinned. "I hope he wasn't mad."

"'T'warn't that so much," said Charlie. "What kind of irritated him an' his friends was havin' to keep their hands up. I didn't see no point in it myself. But you know how Doc is when he takes a notion. He 'lowed as how it was a health measure. If you ain't used to it a hour passes long thataway."

Doc Grimson glanced back at the canyon mouth, where it widened out into the valley. "You boys get right along with the cattle," he said. "Charlie and me want to rest here. We'll join you at the Flyin' M Bar."

The three got along with the cattle. When they had progressed some five or six yards, they heard a couple of shots behind them in the canyon, followed by a sharp fusillade. After that there was silence.

Lance grinned in the darkness. "I reckon Ogalally's decided to make camp," he said.

Several miles from the other end of the canyon, where a cottonwood-bordered stream meandered down the long slope, they themselves made camp. It would be difficult to move the cattle away from the water in the morning but it would have been even more difficult that night, and the animals were tired and thirsty. Lance did not want to deliver them at the Flying

M Bar exhausted and gaunted. This herd was worth a lot of money at anything but rustlers' prices.

Lance decided that he wouldn't tell old man Hewitt that his son was dead. No use spoiling his happiness at getting the cattle back until it was necessary. But though he tried to think only of the rancher, the face of the girl in the photograph kept coming into his thoughts as he slipped into his soogans. Claire, the boy had said her name was. Not that he, Lance, ever wanted to have anything to do with another woman. Lord forbid! Still, he did not go to sleep right away. He lay awake a long time, looking up at the intricate burning maze of the stars, which looked big and close enough to drop a rope on.

CHAPTER 5
FIGHTING PARDNERS!

IT WAS the next day at noon when Lance and Flint saw the heliograph, if that was what it was. They had gotten the herd in motion at the first streak of dawn and had pushed them hard all morning. Behind them, gaunt orange and purple, the great semi-circle of the rimrock reared, battlemented, sheer, forming a sort of immense fortress for the wild bunch but precluding, too, the possibility of effective pursuit as long as the deep canyon was held.

The glint of light came from the top of the rock several miles from the gap which showed the location of the canyon. None of the three could make out the message and the flickering stopped only a few seconds after they first saw it. Had it only just begun, or had it been going on for some time behind their backs before they halted?

Lance thought he saw an answering flash from the hills in front of them, but he could not be sure.

Flint shook his head thoughtfully as he and Lance exchanged glances.

"May be nothing," Lance offered, optimistically.

"Maybe," said Flint, "but I'm thinkin' we better keep an eye peeled for trouble and plenty of it. Who else but Ogalally would be sending messages by flashing a mirror from that rimrock. He must be sending word to somebody to cut us off."

Lance sat in silence for a moment, then he said. "They'll have to hurry, an' we're back-trailin'. Before sundown we'll be at the turn-off of the trail where we came in from Mexico. Instead of turning off, we go on maybe two hours drive across that broken country and we get on the main trail across the high mesa. There's a big spread there and plenty of goin' and comin' on the trail. If Ogalally's signaling to some pals of his, they'll have to hit us before sundown. Once we get over the rough country we'll be in easy striking distance of help. They'll know they can't get away with a herd this size when an hour's fast ride will start a posse on their trail."

"There's lots of time until sundown," Flint pointed out.

Lance hunched his shoulders cheerfully. "The light'll be good for shootin'," he said, grinning.

And at sundown trouble came. The herd had just reached the turn-off which led down into Mexico, when, around a bend, a group of riders came into view. They were sitting motionless in the trail, a compact group of six or seven men. Lance, riding point, saw them first and whirled his pony to let the others know. At his signal Flint and Lockjaw rode towards him, while he turned back toward the group on the trail. They had not moved.

He wondered. Were they waiting for him to come to them? Or were they there on other business and not interested in him?

Characteristically, he rode straight towards them. The best thing to do was to find out. The fact that they outnumbered him seven to one made no impression on him. Lockjaw and Flint were behind him. Casually, he loosened his guns in his holsters as he jogged ahead.

The first rider, in front of the group, was a tall, heavy, red-bearded man, with a great fleshy beak of a nose and a cast in one eye. Lance didn't like him. He didn't like any part of him. He looked bad; he looked as though he could be trusted about as far as you could throw a bull by the tail. But it wasn't that which made Lance hate him at sight. It was just one of those immediate antagonisms which spring up between certain types of men. At sight they, just naturally, hated each others' guts.

The riders grouped behind the big man looked just about as bad in their ways as their leader did; hard-looking, cold-eyed and ugly. They were dressed like punchers, but the mark of the hired gunman was on them. Being among them was like being among a nest of full-grown rattlers. But Lance barely glanced at them. It was the big man who had his hackles rising like a prodded game-cock.

"Where'd you get them cattle?" this man demanded harshly as Lance drew up in front of him.

"Who wants to know?" Lance rapped back at him.

The big man sneered, "Now don't get proddy, sonny." It was plain that he wasn't impressed by the slim-hipped, wide-shouldered, blue-eyed youngster before him. "We know them critters are rustled and we're here to take them and you too. So keep your hands well away from them two guns I saw you loosening up out there, or you'll get yours plenty and quick."

Lance's eyes narrowed. "Howcome you know they're rustled, mister?" he asked sharply.

FOR THE split part of a second the big man looked discomfitted but he recovered quickly enough. "We can see the brand, that's howcome!" he thundered.

"You're kind of jumpin' to conclusions, ain't you?" Lance drawled. "You ain't seen many of 'em. What were you waiting here for anyway?"

"That's enough talk out of you," the leader snarled. "Get your hand over your head and start prayin' you get jail instead of a noose."

Lance laughed harshly. "Look over my shoulder, mister," he said, "and you'll see a couple of gents back there aways with Winchesters over their arms. Neither one of 'em knows how to miss. The first man in your bunch who goes for his gun will be the first to die, but not the last. *Comprende?*"

The big man flushed. "Goin' to make a fight of it, are you?" he sneered.

"Maybe. You weren't countin' on just that, were you? You

thought we'd all three crowd up under your guns, didn't you? Ogalally ought to have taken time to signal you that we weren't that dumb."

"I'm givin' you one last chance," the leader snarled. "Either explain where you got them cattle or get your hands up and call to your partners to come in peaceable."

"Well, at that, I think I'll tell you," Lance said, eyeing him ironically. "The cattle are rustled all right—rustled from Ogalally Pete. We're driving them back to Hewitt at the Flying M Bar where they belong."

"That's a story too." The leader's one straight eye took on an expression of craftiness and cruelty. "You think anybody's likely to believe it?"

The big man raised his left hand to his hat and took it off. As he did so, something in his eyes gave Lance a split-second premonition of the truth, but the impression came too late. The man's horse leapt suddenly as though stung and there was the immediate report of a rifle from the rocks to one side. At the same instant Lance saw the leader start his draw, was dimly aware that there had been other shots and that his horse was sinking to his knees. His right hand flashed holsterward and came away belching fire, but his falling mount spoiled his aim. The bullet meant for the big man's middle struck the gunman's weapon just as it cleared leather, and drove it against the nose of one of the horses behind him. The horse reared wildly.

Lance cleared the saddle in a sudden wide leap, landed crouching as lead whipped around him. His gun cracked again and this time there was nothing to spoil his aim. One of the crowd whose bullets were searching him out, reeled in the saddle and slumped to the ground.

All this had taken place in the space of seconds. He saw another saddle emptied at the same instant, and then found himself the center of snorting, frightened cattle which were trying to stampede in all directions at once. The steers served to shield him from further bullets but that maddened sea of horns and hoofs became suddenly more dangerous than flying lead. Crowding between the flank of one steer, and the flailing horns of another, Lance vaulted over the first steer's back, dodged another and flung himself on the back of a third to escape the horns of a fourth. The steer bucked wildly, but for crucial seconds Lance managed to stick. He was aware, with a faint sensation of astonishment, that the other crowd were galloping off, keeping low in the saddle and urging their horses to a dead run.

Something struck with a vicious thud near him and the yearling he was riding gave a few last frenzied bucks which carried it to the side of the trail where at length it managed to dislodge its rider. Lance landed head over heels on the hard ground at the trail's edge, and lay for a second with the breath half knocked out of him. A lead slug whipped into his shoulder like the sting of an angry wasp; another smacked dirt into his face. He got to his feet fast and ran dodging for some low rocks which lay fifty yards to his rear. As he ran he heard a shout from that direction. Flint was already there and he saw Lockjaw running toward them.

Bullets whipped around Lance, but his swift zigzag progress made a difficult target. He arrived untouched at just about the same time that Lockjaw did. Flint was working with his rifle, firing at the faint puffs of smoke which came from the slope above them.

"What the hell happened?" Lance panted. "Who are these jaspers on the slope?"

"Same gang," Flint explained between shots. "It was a trap.... That skunk you were talkin' to must have give the signal when he took off his hat.... They shot all three of our horses first off.... Since then, they been shootin' at us. The others high-tailed it and stopped behind that shoulder in the trail up there.... They're fannin' out now to throw in with their pardners."

Lockjaw said nothing. He was busy with his rifle. LANCE COULD see figures on the slope some distance down the trail, dodging from cover to cover, working around to good rifle range of where they lay. As he watched, one of them threw up his arms and fell forward; the rifle he carried describing a slow arc through the air before it, too, hit the ground.

"Bet I got him plumb through the heart," said Lockjaw with satisfaction.

Lance looked at him and grinned involuntarily. If Lockjaw was even vaguely excited he gave no sign of it. He levered his Winchester with a leisurely hand and sighted with great de-liberation. Except for a faint expression of pleasure around the eyes, his long heavy features were as wooden as usual. A bullet struck a rock in front of him and drove splinters into his face. One cut his cheek open just beneath the eye. Lockjaw shook his head and brushed a hand across his face with the abstracted impatience of a marksman bothered by a random fly. He sighted again and squeezed the trigger, watching the effect of his shot with narrowed eyes.

"I believe that there wind," he observed slowly to Flint, decorating the nearby rock with a brown squirt of tobacco juice, "I believe that there wind is stronger up on the slope."

"Yeah," Flint answered, absorbed, "It's hard to allow for."

Lead smacked at the rock in front of Lance. He turned his head and swore. A couple of men had worked around to the high ground on their side of the trail. They were surrounded.

That made it hopeless. The rocks among which they lay were really no cover against rifle fire from the high ground on either side. It was simply a question of time before they were picked off, one by one. All that had saved them thus far was the fact that their attackers had to shoot from a long range and had not gotten it yet. After a little, though, they would pick it up, and that would be the end of the game.

Lance cursed himself for the blind over-confidence which had let him, with the others, be trapped here. He felt like apologizing to his partners. He had gotten them into this. Even his Winchester lay a hundred yards away near his dead horse. It had been a good trap, all right. That big, fat, cock-eyed rattler had made a fool out of Lance!

"Listen, fellas," Lance said suddenly. "I'm sorry for this. I acted like a fool. We'd better take a chance on givin' in. It's boothill for us sure, the way it is now."

Flint smiled at him. "Forget it. You couldn't help it. An' it's no use sayin' we got a belly-full. Three of 'em are dead. All they'd do is to hang us now. We just got to play out our string."

Lockjaw grunted. " 'T'ain't yore fault, Lance," he said, awkwardly. "It was me killin' that cat, I reckon. I'm shore sorry for it."

Flint snorted, "Hell! We ain't dead yet."

A man on the opposite slope stood up suddenly and fell forward, draped over the rock in front of him.

"I thought so," said Lockjaw, mildly triumphant. "There's right smart of wind up there. I was holdin' anyways three inches to the left of that feller's head."

Lance's heart warmed suddenly. He suggested quitting because he had gotten them into a fight and he wanted to get them out of it. He hadn't expected them to agree. What partners for any man!

Well, that was four of them gone. There couldn't be more than seven or eight left. He got up on his hands and knees.

"Where you goin'?" Flint asked.

"Down to get my rifle," said Lance calmly.

"Don't be a fool!"

"Shucks! Those rannies can't shoot good enough to...." He broke off suddenly. Three figures had appeared on the trail. He watched two of them ride forward at a fast lope, motioning the third to remain behind. But the third disregarded the signals, and as the distance decreased Lance saw suddenly that the third rider was a girl.

CHAPTER 6
SHADOW OF THE NOOSE

L ANCE DROPPED down again. His vision cut off by the rocks he could not see that the two men had ridden forward until they were in plain sight of those of the slopes. The man in the lead reined in his horse and held up his hand authoritatively. His voice came faintly. "Lowery! Ed Lowery!" he called. The sun caught a glint of metal on his chest as he raised his arm.

"You reckon that there's a sheriff?" asked Lockjaw, whose eye also had caught that glint in the sunlight.

"Reckon so," Lance grunted, his gaze still intent.

Lockjaw said querulously, "Dang if a man can put down his foot in this country without steppin' on one of them sheriffs!" He swung his rifle and settled with it into a comfortable position. "Anyways," he said, "we can shore take care of this one right here and now."

Flint put out a hand and knocked the rifle up. "Wait a minute, you locoed galoot," he said. "This looks like a break —an' we could shore use one."

The firing from the slopes had, in fact, slackened and then ceased.

Flint looked at Lance. "Wasn't Lowery the name young Hewitt told you…?"

"Yeah," the latter returned grimly. "An' Lowery must be the red-whiskered coyote that's leadin' this bunch. Begins to look kind of interestin', don't it?"

41

Flint pointed to the figure of a man circling down, out of rifle range. "There he goes," he said.

The man with the badge on his chest rode back to meet him. There was a brief and apparently sharp colloquy between the two and then the horseman rode forward again.

"You, in the rocks," he shouted. "This is Sheriff Baker talkin' to you. You'd better give up. You got no chance in there."

Lance locked at Flint, who said: "He'd bring a posse while these others held us here. Better make a talk for it. We can't expect Doc and Charlie along before morning. They'll keep holding that pass to be sure we got plenty of time."

Lance nodded agreement. He yelled to the sheriff. "We got your word for it that nothin' happens to us without a regular trial?" he asked.

"That's it," the sheriff shouted. "Come on in."

The three got up and walked over to him. The men on the slopes did likewise. Lance saw that the girl had cantered up from the rear. As he neared her his heart jumped. He had become certain of what he had dimly suspected before. The girl was Claire Hewitt.

Lance opened verbal hostilities as soon as he got in talking distance. "I'd like to ask these hombres what they mean by cutting down on us from ambush after I explained that we were drivin' these cattle to the Hewitt spread," he said sharply.

Red Ed Lowery blustered. "It's a lie! These fellers started the shooting, and there lie two of my men to prove it!"

The sheriff glowered suspiciously at Lance. "How are you explainin' that?" he challenged.

Lance told his side of the story, adding: "If you don't believe that, we're willin' to act it out for you again—if this Lowery liar is willin' to show his draw against mine again, and take the consequences!"

Lowery flushed with rage. "That's a fine story," he said. "Ask any of my men if it ain't a lie out of whole cloth. The truth is that these fellers rustled Hewitt's critters and have been holdin' them up in the hills until they found a market for 'em. Today they was drivin' 'em into Mexico. Right here's where the Border trail turns off. They thought they could slip through without anybody seein' them, or else bluff it out and run the cows through, anyhow. Just by luck we was too many for 'em—that's all there is to it! It's got to a fine pass when you'll listen to a low-down rustler lie against a known stockman!"

"Easy—easy," the sheriff cautioned him. "Nobody's said anything about takin' these hombres' word for anythin'. I'm the sheriff of this county and it's my duty to listen to what they got to say. Words ain't goin' to hurt anybody."

"Yeah," Lance put in sardonically, "don't lose your head, Lowery. You've already lost the cattle—no use givin' yourself away."

Lowery's face purpled, but before he could find speech Lance prodded him again. "You was goin' to dry-gulch us and take the cattle for yourself, wasn't you? And now you're pretty sore because the sheriff happened along and blocked your play. So you're fixin' to get us jailed to save your face. What the hell were you doing here, anyway, Lowery?"

THE BIG ranchman looked purple-faced with anger, but

controlled himself by obvious effort. He was shrewd enough to realize that this was a crucial question.

"Why the hell should I explain anythin' to this murderin' rustler, Baker," he said, with a semblance of reasonableness, "but since he's brought the question up I might as well tell you. Some more of Hewitt's and my cattle was rustled last night. We're gettin' pretty tired of it. The trail was lost in the barrens, like it always is, but before it was lost it was leadin' down into Mexico. It suddenly come over me that that direction might be a blind—that the cattle was really run somewheres else. So I got my men and fogged out here, cuttin' for sign. We didn't find the stuff we was after, but you can see for yourself that I guessed right. These critters haven't been in Mexico—they been held somewheres in the mountains yonder."

Lance laughed, simulating a confidence he didn't feel. Lowery's story sounded convincing. "Good yarn, Lowery!" he applauded. "But it won't do. Ogalally Pete signaled you with that helio and you came to get *this* herd. A man doesn't go out cuttin' for sign he's got no reason to think he'll find, and drag ten or twelve men with him, all loaded for bear. You and Ogalally are in cahoots, and you have been all along. I don't know why you've set yourself to steal the Flying M Bar blind, but I know you have been doin' it—and young Bill Hewitt knows it, too!"

The girl started. Her hand went suddenly to her throat. "You—you've seen, my brother?" she asked.

Lance's eyes softened. "Yes, ma'am," he said, impulsively, "and he sent something to you by us." He reached into his pocket and drew out Bill Hewitt's wallet. "He asked me to bring this money to you," he said gently.

Ed Lowery's one straight eye narrowed to a wolfish gleam. "What did he send his pocketbook for?" he asked suddenly.

Lance's heart sank and his stomach suddenly felt leaden, sick. He had done it again. Only this time he had betrayed them all irrevocably.

"Why—why," he got out, "he had had a little accident and...." The desperate consciousness that every word he said damned him more completely thickened his tongue and brought the guilty color to his cheeks.

Lowery said with a wolfish grin, "We can just about guess the kind of accident he had—the kind of accident that would make him give you his *pocketbooks* as well as his money." Suddenly he thundered: "You murderin' skunk! You killed Bill Hewitt and now, knowin' you're going to be searched, you're taking the only way you know to get rid of the evidence. Sheriff, I demand that you arrest these men for cattle stealin', for the cold-blooded killin' of my riders—and for the murder of Bill Hewitt!"

The girl's hand was pressed to her heart now and her face white. Her eyes, fixed on Lance, were wide with incredulous horror. Lance groaned, for once in his irrepressible life bereft of speech.

Flint Maddox said calmly, "Murder must be in your line, you sway-backed hawg—you're so quick to see it where it ain't. Bill gave us his pocketbook so as to identify us. Otherwise there wouldn't be nothin' to let his father and sister know that we wasn't tryin' to run some kind of a sandy on them."

The girl said in a choked voice: "For God's sake tell me the truth—is my brother—is he alive?"

Flint said gravely: "He was alive when we last saw him, ma'am."

Lance threw him a glance of gratitude, and some of the horror went out of the girl's eyes. It was as though she believed him just enough to take the dagger from her heart.

"Tell me," she said, "you wouldn't, couldn't lie to me about this—was he badly hurt? Will he live?"

Flint's lean, melancholy, honest face contained no expression other than sympathy. "His horse fell with him, ma'am," he lied tranquilly, "and he was hurt pretty bad. But he's having the best of care, and he told us to tell you not to worry about him."

"Oh!" the girl gasped her relief. "I must go to him—tell me where he is."

"It's a long way from here, ma'am," Flint told her, "and for that reason he didn't want you to come. He made us give our word not to tell where he was. He said he knew you'd want to come—an' he thought it wasn't needed."

Surprisingly Lockjaw spoke. "That's right," he said, a glow of enthusiasm in his eyes, "an' we ain't never broke our word—never, ma'am."

Lance looked at him in humble amazement. Lockjaw—the unpredictable—had said the right, the tactful thing! And then he realized that it had been by accident. Lockjaw had simply stated, with honest pride, the simple truth. They never broke their word. Lockjaw never could get any general conception of right and wrong! He learned his ethics piecemeal, but once he had learned one point he never forgot it. This was a point he had learned. It had come out of him at that moment by a kind of sublime accident. And Lance could see that the girl was comforted. Something in her feminine perception looked into Lockjaw's simplicity and saw that he spoke the truth. What that truth represented, however, she mercifully did not know. And would not know—though all three hanged to keep it from her.

The sheriff, however, was not endowed with feminine perceptions. The story was too thin to suit him. He threw a pitying glance at Claire, then said gruffly: "Git goin'. Walk ahead, you three. Lowery, send one of your boys ahead, will you, to get some horses for 'em. I want to get them to jail sometime before morning."

CHAPTER 7
LOOP FOR A LAWMAN!

HORSES WERE obtained from the nearby ranch, and the three mounted, their saddles having been taken off their dead mounts and brought along.

Lowery and two of his men went along with the sheriff and his deputy while the remainder stayed back to drive the cattle. Claire Hewitt, to the surprise of everyone, rode with the sheriff's party.

She herself scarcely knew why she made that decision. Nor-

47

mally, she would have thought it her duty to stay with the Flying M Bar herd, even though Ed Lowery assured her that his men would take care of them. But there was something very curious in the whole situation surrounding the three captives. Their charges against Lowery, the latter's ill-concealed fury, the fact that they brought her bother's wallet.... It was true the case against these three looked very bad. Was she to believe that they really were murderers as well as cattle thieves? Something in her protested vigorously at the idea.

She looked at them as they rode before her, hands bound behind them. Even their backs were the backs of honest men, she thought suddenly. They held themselves straight and rode proudly. They looked clean and hard and entirely unafraid. That wasn't the way captured murderers would look.

All at once she became aware of something one of the men was doing. He was working to free his hands—under the very eye of his captors! It was an almost imperceptible movement, gauged to correspond to the movement of his horse—a flexing and tensing of the muscles of his wrists. That was the young man, the one they called Lance. Would the sheriff and Lowery see it? Should she speak up and tell them?

She remembered again the candor of his face and eyes. He had looked young yet strangely hard and mature at the same time. More than mature, when he talked to Lowery, but his blue eyes had been shy when they looked at her. She recalled suddenly that there had been a photograph of herself in Bill's wallet. Had her brother taken it out and kept it, or had.... She flushed a little and made herself think of the other two—that man with the melancholy face which lighted up so brilliantly when he smiled, and the big, horse-faced man who looked dumb, but honest and good. She knew all at once that she liked all three of them and that the real reason she had ridden with them was because she sensed that her very presence might prevent anything happening to them.

She hadn't much confidence in Sheriff Baker. He was honest and could be brave, but he was a little weak, too, and lacking in moral courage. And she knew that if she and the sheriff weren't there Ed Lowery would think nothing of hanging these men to the nearest cottonwood, sure of the approval and applause of everybody who learned of it.

She hoped that Lance would not try to escape. Lowery would shoot him down like a dog. Then she thought she saw the knots on Lance's wrists loosening a little. The flexing and tensing muscles had more play now. Maybe she ought to say something, if only to keep him from being shot. But instead she kept silent and tried to look as though she weren't holding her breath half the time.

Lance worked at his bonds more as a matter of principle than for any other reason. The broomtail he rode wasn't much good. He'd have very little chance of getting away on him. Not, certainly, as long as that bay stallion of Lowery's was around. Anger boiled up again in Lance at the thought of his own dead mount. There hadn't been many horses in the country with as much speed and bottom. Someday he'd pay Lowery out for that.

Flint, he saw, was in much the same case as himself. The

mustang he rode would never enable him to get away. But Lockjaw, unless Lance missed his guess, would have a lot more chance. He was mounted on a roman-nosed splay-footed, bony-looking beast that certainly would never get very far on his looks, but he had a deep chest and long sloping shoulders, under which hard, supple muscles writhed, and those low hocks promised speed. He wondered if Lockjaw knew what he was riding and decided that he probably did. Whatever he might not know, Lockjaw knew horseflesh.

But if Lockjaw knew he gave no sign of it. He looked down in the mouth. Lance guessed that he was still worrying over that unfortunate mountain lion.

"Don't worry, fella," he said. "We'd have gotten caught even if you hadn't shot that varmint. It didn't make any real difference." LOCKJAW SAID nothing and for a time they rode in silence. He was thinking that it was pretty nice of Lance to try to make out that he hadn't done any harm.

After a while Flint said: "I don't see any way out of this, unless we can prove some way that we got those cattle in Mexico."

Lance grinned: "We better send a note down to Don Juan Bautista, please would he come up and testify that we stole the cattle off him?"

Flint returned his grin. "He might tell, too, who he bought them critters off of. That'd help."

Sheriff Baker called, "That's enough talk, you!"

Lance and Flint turned in the saddle and looked at him as though he might have been some kind of a strange insect. Then they turned forward and resumed the conversation as though there had been no interruption.

"Say, won't that little Mex badman get a kick out of it if he ever hears that we did a dance on the breezes over those cattle!"

"Hell! He's probably dead, already. Swelled up with poison and bit hisself to death the minute we got over the Border."

Lockjaw had ceased to listen. An idea had come crashing into his mind. Don Juan Bautista, if he would talk, could save Lance and Flint from hanging. All Lockjaw had to do was to get hold of the Mexican and make him talk. But in order to do that, Lockjaw himself would have to escape.

They were riding down the main street of the town before this process of reasoning had completed itself. By that time, Lance had loosened his bonds so much that he was keeping them on by holding his wrists apart and hoping that no one would notice. But he saw no possibility of getting away. He was between Lockjaw and Flint and all three were now enclosed by their captors who had ridden up to surround them as soon as they had come into town.

Suddenly Lockjaw's horse began to show signs of restlessness and moved sideways, shouldering the animal of the man who held his reins. The puncher swore and kicked at him. The animal jumped sideways and Lockjaw nearly came out of the saddle. Lance and Flint stared at him in momentary surprise. Lockjaw didn't fall off horses, even with his hands tied behind.

"Hey!" Lockjaw yelled to the puncher, "can't you see I'm falling. Push me back, you fool!"

The puncher edged over and put out a hand to catch him by

the shoulder. "You call yourself a rider," he began to sneer, but broke off as Lockjaw's horse, stimulated by the opposite spurs, lunged forward and sideways. Lockjaw's head went down and then bobbed up and sideways in a vicious butting motion. It connected square with the puncher's chin. He reeled, half-knocked out of the saddle, and dropped Lockjaw's reins. Instantly the roman-nosed mustang leapt forward in a wild jump, his rider's spurs deep in his sides.

LANCE HAD seen what was about to happen. He spurred and kneed his own horse into a sudden whirl, which startled the mounts of Lowery and the sheriff, and slipped his hands from his loosened bonds. At the same instant two six-guns blazed almost in his face. He had a glimpse of Lockjaw, his mount on a dead run, turning a corner into a side street about twenty yards ahead. Several more shots rang out as Lockjaw went out of sight but none of them, apparently, took effect. The confusion was too great for straight shooting.

Lance's first impulse was to take advantage of the clamor and the running men to make a break himself, but he changed his mind suddenly as he saw Lowery set spurs to the Stallion and take off after Lockjaw, cutting down Lockjaw's lead at every jump. That stallion could outrun Lockjaw's horse and Lowery would shoot him out of the saddle mercilessly. Lance grabbed for the riata which hung at the saddle horn.

That was the quickest loop he had ever built, and even then he was nearly too late. Lowery was already rounding the corner when he threw. He didn't dare try for the man. Instead the rope sizzled out low, the noose aimed for the hind hoofs of the horse.

He heard somebody shout behind him but he paid no attention. Then something viciously hard landed on his head and the light went out in a blinding flash. He had only time to see that loop encircling those flying heels—the prettiest throw he had ever made—before darkness engulfed him. But his hand had already started the dally which was to jerk the stallion to the ground, and the hand finished that dally without his being conscious of it!

Another of Lowery's men had started in pursuit and was following close on his chief at the turn. His horse crashed into the falling stallion and went down in a welter of squeals and flailing hoofs. The scrambling horses blocked the street, and by the time effective pursuit had started, Lockjaw, his hands still tied behind him, was racing to safety under cover of falling darkness.

Flint had done his share by interfering with the puncher who rode on his side and had nearly gotten himself shot for his pains, but he had made no attempt to escape. In his situation it would have been suicide.

The sheriff cursed, flung himself from the saddle, gun in hand, by the side of Lance who had fallen to the ground.

Claire Hewitt, cried out involuntarily. "Oh! Is he—did you kill him?" she asked.

The sheriff stopped swearing. "'Scuse me, Claire," he rumbled. "I forgot about you. No, he ain't dead. I'd *ought* to have shot him, though—would have, I reckon, if you hadn't been here."

CHAPTER 8
A GIRL WHO NEEDS HELP

CLAIRE RODE home that night with Ed Lowery. She had not wanted to, but it had been impossible to refuse. The big ranchman had fallen clear of his horse and had come out of the fall with nothing more serious than a bad jar which had knocked the wind out of him. His puncher had not been so lucky. He had gotten a badly bruised shoulder and a couple of smashed ribs.

For the first few miles they rode in silence. Lowery appeared to be chewing the cud of his bitterness and fury. Claire had seen murder in his eyes when he picked himself up and came, gun in hand, to where Lance still lay unconscious. She had stood between the two her back to the prone stranger and Lowery had been helpless. But she felt certain that had Lance been on his feet at that moment nothing on earth could have prevented the rancher from shooting him.

She knew, too, that her own attitude had been a bitter pill for Lowery to swallow. She had insisted on bandaging Lance's head, which the sheriff's gun-barrel had ripped open, and ministered to him until he came to. Lowery had remarked angrily that she showed a lot of tenderness for her brother's murderers, and she had replied sharply that there was yet no proof that they were that. Then the rancher had had the wisdom to clamp his mouth tight until he was able to speak more softly.

At that, Claire scarcely understood herself. She rode those first few miles with her head in a whirl. All she was certain of was that she did not believe Lowery's charges. Now, as she rode, she kept remembering Lance's eyes when he came to and found her bending over him. They had looked as though he were unable to believe his good fortune. The look had embarrassed her suddenly and she had dropped her gaze, flushing.

But when consciousness of where he was and what had just happened came back to him, Lance's first question had been for Lockjaw. "Did he get away?" And at the news that he had the enthusiastic boyish grin had broken out over his face and he had sunk back. "Some man, that Lockjaw," he had remarked happily.

His attitude had done something to Claire. She had become suddenly and vividly aware of the steadfast loyalty that existed between these men. They thought first of each other. She sensed a friendship between them which tightened her throat when she thought of it. The quickness and fearlessness with which Lance had thrown that rope, ignoring his own chance to escape, brought, even in retrospect, a quick glow of admiration to her eyes.

Lowery broke the silence in a surly voice. "Now that your stock's back," he said, "Maybe you think your troubles are over."

Claire said: "Not quite. But it helps." Then she added: "Thanks to you." She tried to make her tone pleasant.

It occurred to her all at once that she had been ungracious enough with Lowery. After all, it was quite possible that she was wrong about Lance and his friends. The cattle might not have been returned if it hadn't been for Lowery.

Lowery softened. "If you'd only make up your mind to marry me, Claire," he said, "all your troubles would be over."

Claire thought: Or just beginning. Aloud she said, "I thought we had all that settled. Let's don't begin it again—please." Again she sought for tone which would soften the refusal as much as possible.

"I can't forget about it, Claire," Lowery said. "I keep thinkin' about it all the time. Listen—hasn't it ever seemed to you that somebody—some gang, maybe—is workin' against your dad? This ain't the end of it. Whoever rustled them critters in the first place ain't goin' to give up now. They're goin' to strike again." His voice became pleading. "Give me the right to take care of you and fight for you. I know you don't think you love me now, but that'll come. I—I'll wait. Only just marry me now—so's I can see you around the house. So's I can call you my wife an' take care of you."

Claire didn't know why she had no emotional response to this plea. She should, she thought, be touched, and at least grateful. But there was something about Lowery which repelled her, and she found that the softer he got toward her the more repugnant he seemed.

"You—you make it hard for me," she told him, in a voice which sounded strained, almost choked, because of the conflict between her dislike and her wish not to hurt his feelings. LOWERY MISUNDERSTOOD. He thought that her resolution had weakened and that now was the time to drive for a decision. He hadn't a very high opinion of women. They liked to shilly-shally and get a man worked up. What they needed then was handling. You had to show you were a man—go after them hard and close the deal. He never had believed that a girl like this could really want to refuse a man like him; not, at least, when she was in danger of being broke. She must know which side her bread was buttered on. He spurred his horse close to hers and clutched her in a strong arm.

Claire was taken by surprise. She found herself suddenly swept against him. His beard swept her face; she felt the avid wetness of his mouth against her cheek. For a second horror and unbelief froze her, then in an automatic gesture she pushed furiously free, and swung her quirt hard against his face.

Lowery cursed, his voice thick with fury. "You—you—" he ground out.

Claire cried with almost equal vehemence: "How dare you? How dare you? My father will kill you for this!"

"Let him try!" Lowery snarled. "I'll fix the lot of you—your fool of a father and you and your crook of a brother!"

For a moment the full import of his words did not reach the girl. Then she flamed with a new cause for anger. "What do you mean by that?" she demanded. "Calling my brother a crook?"

"Because he is one," the rancher answered savagely. "Because he's an outlaw. You little fool—don't you know he's joined up with Ogalally Pete?"

The girl shrank back. "Oh!" she cried. "It's not true!"

"It is true, and I can put him behind the bars any time I want. He's one of the gang that held up the Leadtown stage, and I've got the evidence to prove it!"

"How do *you* know so much about it?"

Lowery rode closer. "I get to know a lot of things," he said, and his voice was cruel. "Now listen, I'm tired of bein' made a fool of. You marry me, or I'll put that young fool in jail where he belongs. You marry me or I'll smash your fool of a father. I'll have you crawlin' to me on your knees and then *maybe* I'll marry you—do you understand?"

Terror-stricken, the girl listened. So this was the man she had tried to force herself to look on as a friend! But though fear held her speechless, her mind was racing. Was it true, what he said about Bill? And could he prove it? If so…. The thought of her brother behind bars—and her father broken and disgraced was more than she could face. Somehow she must save herself, and those she loved as well.

"You—you are sure of this?" she asked weakly.

The ranchman laughed brutally. "Would I be talkin' about it if I wasn't sure?"

"Then—I suppose I—" Claire faltered. "Oh, this is so terrible and unexpected. You must give me time to think."

Lowery said: "You'd better do your thinkin' fast." He sounded triumphant.

"You must give me a little time—a week or two," Claire said softly. "You don't really want me like this. You must give me time to get used to the idea—Ed. It will be so much better for us both."

It was the first time she had ever used his first name. The man could scarcely restrain himself. But he was already conscious that he had lost his head and made mistakes; had talked too much for one thing. It might be better to let the play ride as it was. His bluff was working. Better not crowd it.

"All right," he said at length, "I'll give you three days. But I won't wait any longer."

"Thank you," she said, striving to make her voice sound soft and grateful and loathing herself for it. "I—I'll see you in three days. I must be by myself now, to think."

She turned her horse quickly and set spurs to him. Lowery called after her and started to follow but then thought better of it.

CLAIRE ALMOST killed her pony getting home. But when she came to the last mile she had decided that she must say nothing of all this to her father, so she pulled the lathered mount down, to a walk. Her father would, she felt sure, go after Lowery with a gun and she knew he was no match for the red-bearded man. He would be killed. She must say nothing; she must find some other way out.

Her father greeted her with his face shining. The herd had been driven in just half an hour before and Lowery's men had told him the story of its recapture from the supposed rustlers.

The elder Hewitt was a big, grizzled kindly looking man, ordinarily not inclined to much expression of his feelings, but tonight he was jubilant. In response to his eager questions Claire told him all that had happened until the time she left town.

Hewitt was inclined to think she was mistaken in Lance and the others. "They stole the cattle, any way you look at it," he said. "Either from me or from the man who rustled them in the first place. It ain't likely they'd be bringin' them back here.

An' it don't seem likely that a neighbor like Lowery would be doin' anythin' but try to get 'em back for us. I don't always just cotton to Ed, but Ed's a cattleman himself. He wouldn't do nothin' like that."

Claire could see, however, that what chiefly worried him was the possible fate of Bill. "I'll go into town tomorrow," he said slowly. "Maybe they'll tell me where my boy is." He didn't say what he evidently was thinking, that he had little hope of seeing his son again.

Claire, watching the joy die out of his face, hated the need of telling him anything at all to spoil his happiness in getting the cattle back. She hated, too, to let him take Lowery's side against the others—but she did not dare to tell him what had happened between the ranchman and herself that night.

Now that the excitement of the afternoon and evening was over Claire's spirits sank. It had looked for a moment as though their luck had changed for the better, but now things looked worse than ever. They had the cattle back, it was true—but for how long? Lowery's words rang in her ears: "Whoever rustled them critters in the first place ain't goin' to give up now. They're goin' to strike again." He had sounded curiously positive; did he know something? Was he in it himself? If so, she thought with her heart leaden, then she had better marry him after all. He was too strong for her father to fight.

Once her mind started on this toboggan there was no stopping it before it landed deep in despair. The room had grown very still, but it was a stillness without peace. Neither of them could find anything to say. Claire watched the lined mask of her father's face, deep-etched in the lamplight. It held no expression. Only the set of the mouth and the occasional angry flare in his eyes told her what he was thinking of—his son whom he feared dead, and of the men who had killed him.

As she looked at him a blank, heavy despair swept down on the girl. Her limbs felt heavy, as though she could not lift them, even though she wished to. But there was in her, too, an odd, contrary sense of expectancy. A part of her waited for something she knew would happen—she could not imagine what. But it was there—a strange sense of excitement in the back of her head, keeping time to the measured tick of the clock, throbbing against the emptiness of despair as the clock sounded against the deep silence of the room.

And then suddenly that silence was broken by a sharp knocking on the door. Claire sat forward with her rapidly beating heart, her limbs alive.

Her father got up looking with an exclamation of surprise. There had been no preliminaries, no warning sounds preceding the knock. He stood, hesitant a moment, half started toward the door, then reached to the wall beside where his gun belt hung. He buckled it on, looking a little shame-faced as he did so.

"Come in," he called.

The door swung open. Two men stood there; one in advance, his figure clear in the light, the other behind him, half-obscured. The man in front was a slender, gray-eyed man, grizzled about the temples, with a bold, finely-shaped nose and a sensitive, mobile mouth. Of the other Claire could see beneath the shadow of his sombrero, nothing but a square chin covered with skin like finely wrinkled leather and topped by a flowing white mustache.

CHAPTER 9
COLT CHALLENGE

HER FATHER said: "Good evenin'." His voice sounded stiff.

"You're Hewitt, are you?" the slender man asked.

"That's my name," her father told him, "but I reckon you've got the advantage of me."

"Grimson is my name," the slender man told him, "and this is my partner, Charlie Parr. We're looking for three friends of ours who were driving some of your cattle back to you. Haven't they gotten here yet?"

Hewitt looked grim. "So you're the other two," he said slowly. The two that were supposed to be holding off Ogalally Pete and his gang."

"I guess that answers my question," Doc told him smiling. "It's evident that they've gotten here. Where are they now?"

"They're in jail," Hewitt answered, still grim.

Doc Grimson's eyes went suddenly cold. "That needs some explaining," he remarked. "Suppose you begin. Did you have them put in jail?"

"No," Hewitt told him, his voice hard, "I didn't have that pleasure. I don't reckon I'd have been that easy on 'em."

Charlie Parr laughed shortly, "I told you this was foolishness," he drawled. "The shorest way I know to git in trouble is to run around tryin' to help some fool what cain't tend to his own business. I never got nothin' out of it yet, except a kick in the pants an' no thanks from anybody."

Claire looked at him, and knew all over again that she had been right to trust the others. His words had sounded as though he were regretful and complaining, but his manner denied it. He exuded a great calm and placidity. He made you believe that he had never been really ruffled in his life.

Claire cut in quickly. "It happened through a misunderstanding, I think," she said, smiling warmly. And she went on rapidly to explain what had happened.

The pair heard her out in silence. When she had finished Doc whistled softly. "Helioed Lowery, did they!" he commented. "Well, well! That'll bear some thinking over."

Her father had once or twice tried to interrupt her but she had rushed on. Now when her father spoke the anger was clear in his voice.

"Suppose you tell me where my son is," he challenged, his voice trembling despite himself.

"You heard what your daughter said," Doc said gently. "We gave our words not to tell."

"And that's a likely story! Do you expect me to believe it?"

Doc Grimson continued calm. "The story's true, Hewitt," he said. "You're putting yourself on the wrong side of the fence. Can't you see that Lowery's the man you want to go after? We're only in this because we wanted to help you out."

"Enough palaver!" Hewitt said. He was almost choking with

anger. "Do you take me for a fool? Damn you, *Where's my boy? What have you done with him?*"

"Dad, please!" Claire protested.

Her father waved her to be silent. Doc said, with an edge to his voice: "I'm tryin' to be patient with you Hewitt, because I know how you feel. Don't push it too far."

Claire's face whitened. This quarrel would end in disaster. She had never seen her father like this. Somebody would be killed, and in any case they would lose the help which these two men, she felt, could surely bring them.

"Please, please!" she cried helplessly.

No one paid any attention to her.

"I'm givin' you your last chance, skunk," her father thundered. "Talk up."

Doc Grimson did not move. He simply became immensely still. His hands hanging near the guns in the worn, shiny black holsters, looked as though they were carved out of brown ivory. Claire looked at them in sudden fascination. They looked immensely strong and capable but supple and delicate, too—the hands of a sculptor, or a surgeon, or a magician. And she knew suddenly that her father was very near death.

"Go to hell, Hewitt," Doc Grimson said quietly.

Hewitt's hand flashed to his gun. "Fill your hand then," he gritted.

With a cry, Claire flung herself on him. "Wait—wait, Dad!" she gasped. "I've got something to tell you!"

HEWITT STARED at her blankly a moment as though

he had forgotten her presence. "Say it, then, daughter," he said impatiently, "and then get out of the room."

Neither Doc Grimson nor Charlie Parr had stirred. Breathlessly, the girl told him what had passed between her and Lowery that night.

Hewitt looked dazed. "Is this true?" he demanded at last of Doc and Charlie. "Is he with Ogalally Pete?"

Doc said slowly. "I reckon the cat's out of the bag. Yes, it's true. That's why he made us promise not to tell you."

"Then—then, is it true that he's hurt?"

"He was shot by one of the gang," Doc told him gravely. "He's badly hurt, but he may pull through."

Hewitt groaned. "I've got to get to him," he said.

"You'd never git within a mile of him, even if you could find Ogalally's hideout," said Charlie Parr.

Hewitt straightened his shoulders and reached for his hat. Anger was back in his face. "I'll have a word to say to this crawlin' rattler, Lowery, anyway," he said.

Doc barred his way. "Take it easy," he said. "You won't do any good by landing over there all spread out. You'll only get yourself killed. Let's give this Lowery some rope. He's about to hang himself higher than a kite."

In the end Hewitt let himself be persuaded. "What's your plan?" he asked.

Doc shook his head smiling. "Too early to have one," he answered. "First off, have you got a place for two new riders?"

"Plenty. I had to let my hands go. Didn't have enough cattle left to keep 'em and couldn't pay 'em, anyhow."

"Better sign us on then, and then look for some others."

Claire said thoughtfully. "Do you dare stay around here? If Lowery and the sheriff learn who you are they'll put you in jail with the others."

Charlie Parr chuckled. "Don't worry none about that," he advised her.

Doc Grimson smiled too, but when the girl continued to look doubtful he said:

"They've got no proof of who we are. If we don't tell them they can't even try to jail us."

A shadow of anxiety crossed Claire's eyes. "I'm not sure they would try to put you in jail," she said slowly. "There was ugly talk in town when I left."

Doc Grimson looked at her, suddenly alert. Charlie Parr ran a gnarled hand over his white mustache and cocked a skeptical blue eye at her. "You mean they'd try to string us up without botherin' the law about it?" he asked. And when Claire nodded, he muttered, "I reckon that means then that they was talkin' about lynchin' Flint and Lance."

"I don't think they will, though," she supplemented hastily. "The jail's new and strong. I guess it was mostly just talk. I think Lowery was trying to stir up something like that, from something I heard him say to some men on the street, but he rode home with me, so...." She did not finish.

"He could ride back again, though, couldn't he?"

"Yes," the girl admitted reluctantly, "but I think maybe.... There aren't so many people in town tonight and those who are there are pretty level-headed."

"If there's any chance of that," Hewitt put in, "the big danger'll come tomorrow night. That's Saturday, and a pretty wild bunch get in. They get liquored up, and—"

"What kind of a man is this sheriff?" Doc Grimson asked.

"Baker's all right, I guess," Hewitt told, him slowly. "Honest enough. I don't know if he'd have the nerve to stand up to a crowd, though, especially with Lowery back of them. Lowery runs a pretty high blaze around here."

A shadow of worry darkened Doc Grimson's gaze. "How long since you left town, Miss Claire?" he asked.

"Three hours, anyway. It's fifteen miles, you know, and I've been home some little time."

Doc Grimson frowned. Charlie Parr's wrinkled face set grimly. They got up in silence. "We'll be riding," Doc said curtly. "See you in the morning."

"You—you're going to town?" Claire questioned, her face pale. "Isn't that unwise? If anyone learns who you are, it will only stir people up and make matters worse. It won't help your friends if…." She paused, unwilling to express her thought.

"If we stretch rope?" Charlie Parr asked. "Don't worry any about that, ma'am. If they learn who we are, they'll learn we ain't easy to hang—an' plenty! We'll be seein' you in the mornin'."

Claire watched them out of the door in silence. She had seen a mob in action once and the memory horrified her. But she felt instinctively that nothing she could say would influence these men. As long as they thought their friends were in danger, nothing would stop them.

CHAPTER 10
LYNCH BLUFF

WHEN THE sun awakened her next morning, however, Doc and Charlie were at the ranch, and the house was full of the happy fragrance of coffee and frying bacon. Charlie greeted her from the kitchen door.

"Took your place as cook this mawnin'," he grinned.

"I'm terribly late," Claire told him, trying to sound conscience-stricken and managing only to sound gay. "My! I don't think I ever slept so soundly!"

"Set down," said Charlie. "Breakfast's ready." He stepped to the door and yelled, "Come an' git it or I'll throw it away!"

Her father and Doc came in, the latter looking fresh as paint. Claire stared at him curiously. "You don't look like anyone who has ridden all night without sleep," she said.

Doc merely smiled.

Charlie came in and set a smoking dish of bacon and eggs and another of steak on the table. "Your friend forget to try and stir up a lynchin'," he twinkled at her. "I reckon you had him plumb excited."

Claire looked worried. "He may try it yet," she said.

"Not in the heat of the day," he told her drily. "Sink your pretty little teeth into that there steak. Biscuits'll be brown in a minute." Claire ate with an excellent appetite. These men somehow inspired her with confidence.

That morning the pair spent riding over the spread. After

luncheon they lazed around, cleaning their guns and rifles. Then they rode toward town.

Like most Southwestern cowtowns in the summer months Longhorn spent its days in heat-hibernation. Even the dust-eddies crawled slowly under the hammering heat of the sun. But the western sky was a riot of color when Doc and Charlie arrived. Already the place was waking up; tinny pianos sounding in the honka-tonks; riders dismounting before hitch racks, bent on sluicing the dust from their throats; sounds of chips, of laughter, of curses…. The two tied up their horses behind the Crescent Palace, the main saloon, and began quietly to circulate.

Tonight, they believed, would be the crucial time as far as mob action was concerned. The Saturday crowd would be in with tempers on edge from the heat; and public indignation would be easy to fan into flame. Let another day go past and the whole incident would be forgotten, until the trial revived it. If there was to be a lynching it would have to be tonight.

It did not take them long to realize that hangin' talk was going around, nor was it hard to spot the people who were fomenting mob spirit. Wherever anyone was especially violent on the subject it turned out to he one of Lowery's Lazy L crowd.

"Looks like trouble all right, Doc." Charlie opined.

Doc nodded grimly. "Wonder where that Lockjaw is. He might have had enough sense to go after some of the old crowd. If they come foggin' in here tonight they're goin' to be useful."

Doc shook his head. "We can't count on that, Charlie," he said.

"No-o, reckon not." Charlie sighed. "Well, there ain't no use worryin' about it. When the time comes, we'll lay into 'em and see if we cain't change their minds. Maybe if we go to the sheriff we could talk some backbone into him; and maybe git ourselves swore in as deputies. Failin' that, we might just take the boys out."

Doc shook his head again. "They're too well guarded," he said briefly. "We'd have to shoot, and that'd bring a mob too quickly. Jail's in the center of town and it's all lit up."

"We got to git 'em out some time. You ain't hopin' to prove 'em innocent are you? I figger we got about as much chance of doin' that as a yaller dog has of scratchin' hisself free of fleas."

"Gettin' them out comes later," Doc said curtly. "Our job now is to stop this lynchin'."

"And stoppin' that," Charlie agreed grimly, "is likely to be a man-sized job."

"The way to stop a lynching," Doc said sententiously, "is to stop it from starting. Listen: Lowery's over in this Crescent Palace saloon, and Lowery's the lynching. Maybe we better stop Lowery first-off."

"You figger to kill him? That'll make plenty trouble, Doc."

"There's got to be plenty of trouble, anyway. But I don't want to kill him. Maybe we can bluff him down. He's over there setting them up for the boys who are hot for a hangin'-bee. Haven't you noticed that every time one of his snakes collects two or three gents who are honin' for action, he takes them over to the Crescent? The play's going to start from there when it comes. Maybe we can break it up before it starts.

"Lowery," said Doc Grimson calmly,
"you're more skunk wrapped up in one
package than any man I ever saw!"

Charlie Parr settled his gun belts. Then deliberately he took out one of his Colts after the other, spun the cylinders, and replaced them.

"You've got a head, Doc," he said gruffly. "Come on. It'll maybe take the public mind off Flint and Lance anyway."

"Take it easy, Charlie," Doc cautioned him. "We don't want to go to shooting unless we have to. My idea is to call Lowery and make him back down. If he does, that'll be enough. The crowd'll be busy thinking about that, and also thinking less of Lowery. The lynchin' idea will just naturally die away."

"He's got a half a dozen gunmen over there with him," Charlie Parr pointed out drily. "Maybe he won't back down."

"I've got an idea the gent's yellow," Doc said quietly. "We'll see, anyway."

IN SILENCE they made their way to the Crescent Palace. They lined up unobtrusively at the bar with the others and looked things over. Doc's guess had been right. The saloon was crowded, mostly with riff-raff for whom Lowery was buying drinks. Talk of mobbing the jail was rife.

The pair listened to the talk for a few minutes, then Doc nodded slightly to Charlie. Together they moved toward the big ranchman.

"Lowery," said Doc Grimson, raising his voice slightly, "you're more skunk wrapped up in one package than I ever saw before!"

The ranchman whirled, his face reddening, his hands going automatically toward his guns.

"Keep your hands away from that artillery," Doc advised him sharply, "unless you want to fill a hole in Boot Hill!"

Lowery glared, but he looked a little disconcerted also. There was something about this slender man before him which warned him that the advice not to draw might be good. He looked dangerous; he looked excessively dangerous. Lowery wasn't exactly a coward, but he wanted to live as much as any other man.

"I'm not here to make palaver with any drunken saddle bums," he said and turned his back.

"I'll make all the talk that's needed, Lowery." Doc Grimson's voice was quiet—ominously quiet—but it carried distinctly to every corner of the room. It was that kind of voice. Its clarity wasn't needed, though. After the first words the room had become deathly still.

"You got three good men in trouble on a crooked deal," Doc Grimson went on. "Now you're trying to get them lynched before they put the dead wood on you. You went in to rustle Hewitt's cattle with Ogallaly Pete because you wanted to break Hewitt. When Ogalally signalled you by helio that the cattle had been rustled from him and were on their way back to Hewitt, you rushed with your killers to block the play."

The ranchman had whirled at the first words, his eyes narrowed. Now he broke in: "So you're the other two of the gang!" he blazed. "I'll hand it to you—you've got nerve. But let me tell you something, cattle thief, you'd better keep a close tongue in your head or you'll find yourself hangin' with your partners."

"What you guess I am and what I am, are two different things, Lowery," Doc said evenly. "But don't let's get off the subject. You went out with your killers to dry-gulch the men who were bringing that herd in. You hoped to kill them and then get the cattle back to Ogalally, or into Mexico, where you took 'em the first time. You had hard luck, Lowery, because you took on better men than you are. Now you're afraid of what those men are going to say in court. You want them to die without testifying. But you're in hard luck again, Lowery. They're not going to be lynched—and if they were, you'd never live to see it!"

The ranchman's face purpled. A vein over his temple pulsed. His blunt, puffy fingers twitched spasmodically at his sides, but he had enough shrewdness to see that gun-play was not the answer to this. Curious eyes were on him which would be quick to seize on any misplay and interpret unfavorably to him. None knew better than he that there is no loyalty in a mob.

"You say words, stranger," he challenged, "but words aren't proof. I've got plenty of cattle of my own—a spread five times as big as Hewitt's. What would I want with his cattle? Your talk is fool talk. I'm known here—my word's my bond. There's no man can say I ever pulled a crooked deal. Who are you? What have you got to back you up?"

WITHOUT WAITING for a reply, he turned to the crowd. "I'm talkin' for you men, because most of you are my friends and neighbors. You've got a right to hear the answers, even when it's a case of a thief that's blowin' off to save his partners from what they got comin'. Speak up. If there's any man that knows anything crooked about Ed Lowery, let him say so. An' if there's anybody that thinks I'm in debt or need money so bad that I'd steal cattle to get it, let him come out and say so."

"Don't make a speech about it; you're not running for office," said Doc sardonically. "I didn't say you needed money."

"Then what'd I steal cattle for—for fun?"

Doc rapped out his answer in a voice which carried a sudden

chill. "You stole 'em to break Hewitt—because that was the only way you could get his girl. You were trying to marry her and she'd have nothing to do with you. Last night you tried to use force with her. You even threatened her with losing those cattle again unless she married you! You're not only a rustler and a killer, but you're a crawling yellow skunk, too!"

Lowery stiffened suddenly. His eyes looked murder. His hands tensed and raised, claw-like, ready for the draw.

A short thick-set man, with a brutal face, nudged him sharply. The crowd saw Lowery look at him in surprise and then bend down while the thick-set man, his foreman, Jake Levitt, whispered briefly in his ear. The whisper was low but in the silence of that room those standing near heard it. What Levitt said was: "Look out—that's Doc Grimson. Don't try to draw against him."

Lowery's face lost several shades of color. For a moment he stood at a loss.

But fury came to his aid and he blurted out: "You're a liar.... A rustler and a liar—damn you!"

For a second anger looked out of the frosty gray of Doc Grimson's eyes. Then it passed. "I'm not ready to kill you yet, Lowery," he said. "I'm aiming to give you a chance to hang yourself. I'll say just one thing more to you—keep away from Claire Hewitt. If you ever try to speak to her again, I'll have to kill you before I'm ready."

Charlie Parr turned during this last speech and walked with a leisurely step to the door. Once there, he turned, and said: "Come on, Doc, I cain't stand the smell in here no more."

Doc turned his back calmly and walked to the door. Once there he turned and said: "We'll be somewhere around town, Lowery. If you or any of your rattlers feel an impulse to start anything, take my advice—don't!"

They stepped out. The crowd held its breath. Insensibly men began to drift away from Lowery's vicinity. There would be no lynching that night.

CHAPTER 11
DEATH DEALS THE CARDS

T HE IDEA of a hanging apparently had disappeared, but despite that fact events were moving rapidly—toward trouble. Sheriff Baker, nervous over having Doc and Charlie in the vicinity, doubled the guards at the jail. Public opinion continued to be thoroughly unfavorable to the prisoners.

A certain percentage of the citizens were secretly swayed by Doc's public accusation of Lowery and believed in it, but their doubt of the ranchman could not convince them of the five hard-looking strangers' innocence. It looked to them like a war between rustlers—and in that case any hanging would be a good hanging.

The sheriff, sensing dynamite in the situation, was making every effort to rush the trial. And from that trial there could be only one verdict, for the story of the prisoners was too thin to be believed. Once a verdict of guilty was in, it was a question as to whether the law would be allowed to take its course. It was a good deal more than probable that the citizens of Longhorn County would take justice into their own hands.

Claire had been aroused to admiration and some hope by the news of Doc and Charlie's exploit in bearding Lowery, but in a day or so she became convinced that no real good had been done. Twice she visited Lance and Flint in jail, under the supervision of a sardonic deputy who taunted the pair with the certainty of hanging.

Lance grinned at the girl. "Don't mind him," he said calmly. "He runs off at the mouth like that all the time. It don't mean anything."

But Claire could see that both he and Flint, under their surface ease, were strained. It was odd, she thought, to see these two in jail. They were like a pair of caged hawks—something bedraggled and drooping about them, despite the undiminished fierceness of their eyes and the courage which showed from every gesture. Freedom, untrammeled freedom, was as much a part of them as their features, as the guns which habitually sagged at their thighs.

A sort of quiet desperate certainty began to grow up in her that they would die. There was no way out; no way to help them to escape; no possibility that the law would not judge them guilty.

And Doc and Charlie appeared to be doing nothing. Her questions brought her no satisfaction. Doc was quiet and evasive; Charlie garrulous and uninformative.

"Ever play poker, Claire?" the latter asked, on one occasion when she brought the subject up. "You know, if you're down to your last chips and holdin' a pair of deuces, it ain't a good idea to bet on 'em. A stack of whites don't make a good bluff. You got to sit tight and hope you'll git dealt a real hand before the ante eats you up. But don't you go to worryin'. Our luck ain't run out yet."

But behind the twinkle in his eyes Claire thought she could read anxiety sitting deep in his mind.

That the two were playing some game in the few days which intervened between the arrest and the trial seemed obvious. What it was, Claire could not guess. Doc, especially, was rarely at the ranch. He seemed to have given over his days and nights to long, mysterious rides from which he returned taciturn and grim. She suspected that he was trying to get something on Lowery and was not succeeding.

And that was exactly what Doc was trying to do. At any time of any day he might have been found stretched out in the brush on top of a ridge a mile or so from Lowery's Lazy L ranch-house, with a three-foot marine telescope before him. From this vantage point he could overlook not only the house but all the comings and goings of its occupants and visitors. When night came, he moved down to a nearer spot.

So far, however, only one thing of interest had taken place. On the day after Doc had called Lowery's hand in the saloon a puncher had ridden out into the hills, leading an extra mount and traveling light and fast. The third day at sunset he had come back again. That was all.

Doc waited. He felt pretty sure that Lowery was too impatient a man not to try something fairly soon. Meanwhile the day for Lance and Flint's trial was getting close. Doc and Charlie had already laid their plans for that day, in the event that nothing happened before to alter the situation. They were desperate plans, but the best they had been able to devise. Watching Lowery was merely to fill in the time. It might get results and might not.

ABOUT SUNSET, the day before the trial, something happened which brought Doc up on his elbows, suddenly alert. From a hill some miles away a thin column of smoke began to rise. As Doc watched it, it disappeared and then reappeared three times, in the manner of Indians signaling. He turned his eyes to the house and saw that from one of the upper windows a mirror flashed in the light of the setting sun. After that the smoke disappeared entirely and some minutes later a single rider showed himself briefly before he disappeared into a brushy draw. He was riding toward the ranch. Evidently the signal had told him that the coast was clear.

Before he finally rode out into the open the swift twilight of the desert country had closed down. But Doc was sure, or almost sure, that the rider was Ogalally Pete!

He waited until the darkness was thick enough to cover him, and then he too rode down toward the ranch-house. Several hundred yards away he concealed his horse in a clump of cottonwoods along the creek and continued on foot. His progress was noiseless but rapid. From time to time he paused to listen, then went on.

The Lowery ranch-house was a rambling two-story building—a structure unusual for this part of the country. Around it were grouped barns, bunkhouse and corrals. Doc had noted before that the yard was always brightly lighted by lanterns hung at the side of the buildings or strung from wires between them. The house, on the other hand, appeared dark, the windows carefully shaded.

It was the trick, obviously, of a man who had reason to fear darkness, who intended to keep out intruders and who took no chances of being shot through a window. And now that illumination was going to make the task he had set himself difficult, if not impossible. Watching from the outer darkness he saw that the yard was full of men—an unusually large number of hands for a spread of that size. Hired gunmen! If he were seen tonight, it would take all the speed and skill he had to get him out alive.

Carefully he circled the house toward the barns. Against one of them his glass had shown him a long ladder which formed the basis of his plan for getting into the house. The back of the barn against which the ladder leaned was in shadow, and once behind it Doc moved forward confidently. Too confidently. When he was within ten feet of his objective he trod directly on the prongs of a rake which lay nearly concealed in some loose hay. The rake swung up, struck him a glancing blow on the shoulder, and then fell to the ground. Doc Grimson froze.

A voice from the yard near the barn said sharply, "What was that?"

Another responded, "Bet you it's a coyote sneakin' around. Le's get him!"

Stealthy footsteps moved toward the barn. Doc glanced

quickly about him. There wasn't a scrap of cover within fifty yards. His only chance lay in going around the other corner of the barn, but that would bring him into the light! Even if he weren't seen by anybody else, these two men would probably circle the building....

His eye fell on a slightly darker blotch against the black bulk of the barn and his memory clicked. Through his glass he had seen two lengths of well-casing which stood upright against the wall with a narrow space between them. Swiftly he moved forward. His clothes were dark; he might be unnoticed there. He stepped in, with his back turned, hunching his shoulders to make them fit and putting his hands before him against the barn wall. Then he held his breath and waited.

CHAPTER 12
LOCKJAW RIDES

A T THE corner of the barn the men stopped. Doc knew they were looking around. Then the second man spoke; "Coyote, hell!" he said disgusted. "Musta been a rat."

"Can't see much in the dark," the first man said. "Let's cast out a bit, we might jump him. No rat made that noise."

"You cast out," the other said sardonically, "I'll watch you work."

The first man moved off, while the one who had spoken last wandered over and leaned idly against one of the pipes. He was so close that if he had swung his shoulder a little he would have leaned against Doc's back.

81

Doc barely breathed. It seemed unbelievable to him that a man could stand so near to a living being in the dark and not sense his presence. But the real test would come when the other came back. If he moved directly toward his partner, he would be facing Doc's back all the way. It was impossible not to be seen. An almost irresistible impulse came to him to whirl on the man who stood leaning so near him. With the advantage of complete surprise he could surely get him. And that would save his life, even though it ruined his plan.

He fought the impulse back and kept every muscle still. In a moment he heard the other man coming back.

"Got away, I guess," he said cheerfully.

He came up to within three feet of the other man. Every nerve in Doc's body crisped for instant explosion at the first sound of discovery.

"Yeah," the second man said drily. "Them rats move fast."

The first sounded irritated. "All right, all right," he said, "it was a rat. It was a mouse. It was a danged tarantula, if you got to have it that way. Come on—no use standin' here in the dark."

They moved off. That man had stood four feet from Doc, facing him, and had not seen him!

Slowly, carefully, he relaxed, slipped out from between the two pieces of casing. He listened a moment, then went to the ladder and began to climb. At the top he pulled himself, flat-handed onto the barn roof and took off his boots. Then he reached down, got hold of the top rung of the ladder and pulled. The ladder was long and heavy but little by little the ladder began to come up. He had to work it up with infinite care until finally he had it on the roof.

Cautiously he slipped up to the roof tree and looked over. The roof of the house itself was quite close to the barn, a wing evidently having been added after the barn was built. Would the ladder reach?

He pulled the ladder up to the roof tree and knotted one end of the rope he carried around a middle rung. That would give him leverage to swing the ladder to the roof of the main house.

He was working on the light side of the barn roof now, and would be seen if anybody took the trouble to look. One of the lanterns was strung just below him, however, and threw a shadow on the top of the barn.

He worked an end of the ladder toward the edge of the barn roof, and then got under it on the roof tree and lifted. The other end came up, slowly, then by means of the rope, he began to lower it.

It reached! It reached with not half an inch to spare, but it reached. The end came down on the very edge of the house gutter. Now, if the gutter was only strong enough to hold.... He tested it, cautiously at first and then—a moment later he was on the roof of the house. There he crouched waiting. His next move was to swing down from the gutter into an open window in the second story. He could not do that until the coast was clear.

After a couple of minutes more the two men turned and went back into the bunkhouse. He moved fast then. He let himself down by his hands and then swung his feet inward until they rested on the window sill. An instant later he was in the house.

THE ROOM in which he found himself was dark and he did not investigate it. He felt his way to the door. It opened onto a corridor which was dimly lighted from the hall below. At the foot of the stairs were two closed doors. He crept down and peered through a keyhole until he whirled silently at the sound of muffled voices filtering through the door opposite. He crept over. Through that keyhole he heard the red-headed Lowery talking to Ogalally Pete.

Ogalally was talking gruffly: "You're loco, spreadin' your loop for that girl. That's dynamite."

"Don't worry about that," Lowery growled. "I'll handle her all right. The other comes first."

Ogalally said indifferently: "That's your business, but you're runnin' a pretty-high blaze. If anything goes wrong, they're likely to run you so far that the seat of your pants rub clean through your saddle."

Lowery laughed harshly. "That's how much you know! I got this county by the tail. Baker gets pale around the gills every time I look at him. He knows I can throw him out of his job any time I want to. What he don't know is that I'm goin' to do it, pronto. Then I'll put my own man in an' run things to suit myself. In the meantime, Baker'll do—so long's he don't get too wise."

Ogalally moved toward the door. "Have it your own way, then," he said. "I'll see you day after tomorrow at daybreak. If you get drunk, just remember it's at the water hole by Hewitt's south fence. Don't make any mistake."

Doc moved swiftly toward the stairs and mounted them quietly. He had barely reached the upper darkness when the door opened and Ogalally came out. Silently, he cursed the difficulties which had made him late. What was this about "that girl?" That meant Claire Hewitt, of course. And what was going to happen day after tomorrow at daybreak? Whatever it was, it was to be the day *after* the trial. Evidently Lowery planned to do nothing to interfere with the "vindication" he expected from the conviction of Lance and Flint. Doc set his jaw grimly. If his and Charlie's plan for tomorrow didn't work…!

Nobody was in the yard when he reached the window. He crossed quickly to the barn and then went through the process of getting the ladder back into its place. It was important not to leave any sign of his visit.

Like a shadow, he slipped back to his horse. Ed Lowery and Ogalally would have a little entertainment arranged for them day after tomorrow—at daybreak!

Charlie and Hewitt were still awake when Doc Grimson arrived and recounted briefly what he had heard.

"The skunk!" Hewitt swore. "If he touches a hair of Claire's head….."

"But remember," Doc said, "Lowery told Ogalally: *'that comes later.'* Whatever he's going to try at daybreak day after tomorrow comes first."

"An' what you reckon that can be?" Charlie Parr asked reflectively.

"Maybe it's the cattle," Hewitt said slowly. "Whatever it is, we've got to get the sheriff and have him there to back our play." DOC AND Charlie exchanged glances. The idea of appealing to the law was something difficult for them to stomach at any time, but in this case, they saw that it would be worse than useless. "Baker'd laugh at us," Charlie said. "What proof have we got except Doc's word? He wouldn't believe it, likely, but even if he did he'd pretend he didn't. Lowery wasn't talkin' just to hear himself when he said he had Baker bluffed. From all I can hear Lowery's the big augur around here. You got to get him to rights before you talk."

"Anyway," Doc put in, "We've got a little time. We're going into the trial tomorrow. We hope to see you afterward. If we aren't here by midnight, ride and get the sheriff—if you can."

Hewitt shot him a sharp glance. "You figgerin' on tryin' somethin' at the trial?"

Doc nodded.

Hewitt shook his head. "I hate to see you try it, amigos," he said, looking worried. "You don't know what you're gettin' into. Baker's goin' to be on his guard and the crowd's goin' to be plenty worked up. I was in town this afternoon and feelin' is already beginnin' to run pretty high again. Myself, I'd as soon try to steal a cub bare-handed from a couple of grizzlies than try to take anybody away from that mob.

Doc lifted his shoulders. "We've got to try," he said.

"I wish that danged Lockjaw would turn up," Charlie exploded in sudden irritation. "Blamed if I can figger what's happened to him."

Claire exclaimed: "Oh! I forgot to tell you what Lance said the other day. He said he and Flint had been trying to figure it out, and they remembered that just before Lockjaw made his break they had been kiddin' about the Mexican you took our cattle from—saying that if he would just be kind enough to come and testify for them they'd be able to prove their story was true. He said it would be just like Lockjaw to take it seriously and try to do something about it."

Doc thumped his knee. "Why didn't I think of it," he almost shouted. "That's where he's gone sure as fate. It *is* just the kind of fool thing he'd try."

Charlie Parr groaned: "Oh Lord! The jaw-headed hoptoad! As if we didn't have enough trouble. Now we'll have to go down and get him out."

LOCKJAW, THE subject of all this speculation, had ridden straight for Mexico. He avoided all towns, and cut directly for Don Juan Bautista's ranch, rating his horse along so as to get the most speed out of him without tiring him too much. It occurred to him that he would need a fairly fresh horse for what he intended to do. Otherwise it is probable that he would not have stopped either for food or sleep.

In fact, he actually did go foodless. He had no weapons with which to kill even a prairie chicken. He slept while his mount rested, tightened his belt and rode on. It was sundown of the second day when he crossed the road into Mexico and came into sight of Don Juan's ranch.

His plan of action was not complicated. Lockjaw had a simple mind. It contained, as a rule, only one idea at a time. Just now that idea consisted in a conviction, entirely erroneous, that had he not shot that mountain lion his partners would not be in trouble. That being the case, it was up to him, Lockjaw, to get them out. Lance and Flint had said that only the Mexican's testimony could do that; hence he had to kidnap Don Juan. The way to do that was to ride in, throw the man over his pummel and ride off. Nothing simpler. The thought of possible danger to himself never entered his head.

He rode straight for the ranch-house, and as he approached it, his heart lightened. Don Juan Bautista was standing there in the yard. About him were grouped half a dozen or so vaqueros whom he appeared to be haranguing about something. Lockjaw considered this to be great luck. He had been afraid the man might not be at home and so, foolishly, be the cause of delaying the whole project. Also, there were only half a dozen of those fellows around him.

Lockjaw was a little sorry that he hadn't a gun. He had thought it unwise to stop in any town on the other side of the Border to get one, for it was possible that his description had been telegraphed around. And going to the nearest Mexican town would have meant an extra ride of twenty or twenty-five miles. Still, it was a pity he didn't have one, because that would have made the thing pretty simple.

He shook the thought aside and put his horse into a lope. He'd get a gun off one of those vaqueros. They were loaded down with enough artillery to equip an army.

It was just about at this moment that Don Juan Bautista looked up from his speech and recognized Lockjaw, or rather his eyes told him that the approaching *Americano* was one of those five who had rustled his cattle, but his mind declined to credit it. For one of those men to lope calmly into his very yard would have been a serious affront to Don Juan's dignity, hence this thing could not be true. Don Juan had a great deal of dignity. His small, rotund frame was weighted down with it. It bristled from his warlike mustachios, flashed from his eloquent eyes, dripped from his strutting walk—and was in fact the basis of his existence and the cornerstone of his life.

He stared at Lockjaw indignantly, as though with the lightning of his glance he could cause him to disappear. It was not until his foreman, whose mouth had been hanging open in equal incredulity, exclaimed: *"Dios!* It is one of those dogs who stole the cattle!" that Don Juan began to be convinced. At that moment Lockjaw pulled up his horse and slid from the saddle.

His rock-like fist connected with the foreman's jaw while his other hand reached for the gun in the man's holster. Unfortunately the blow was too effective. Instead of dropping the man in his tracks, it picked him up and sent him flying backwards, so Lockjaw missed his reach for the gun.

Don Juan screamed curses, beside himself. "Dog, and son of a dog!" He reached for the six-gun in an ornate holster on his thigh. Lockjaw snapped a left to his face, which sent him reeling but did not knock him out.

Bang! A six-gun exploded almost in Lockjaw's face. Simultaneously someone on his other side let out a yell of pain. The vaquero who had fired had missed Lockjaw but connected with the shoulder of one of his comrades. Lockjaw knocked the gun from his hand as he tried to fire again. Another vaquero rushed him with a knife. Lockjaw kicked him in the stomach. Other men were running, yelling, from the bunkhouse. He heard shouts.

"Qué pasa?" "A Gringo has gone mad! He is trying to kill the *padrone!"* He made a dive for the fallen gun. He got his hand on it but felt a stunning blow on the back of his head as he did so. A vaquero behind him, afraid to shoot because Don Juan was in the line of fire, had clubbed him. Lockjaw staggered to his feet, reeling, the Colt he had reached for still in his hand. The Mexican leapt in and dealt him a smashing barrel blow across the face.

As Lockjaw staggered back, dazed and half-blinded, the gun in his hand spoke once. The vaquero clutched his shoulder and the weapon dropped from his hand. Then another gun bellowed, three times in quick succession. Lockjaw's head exploded in a great blaze of light. That was the last he knew of that fight.

CHAPTER 13
SUDDEN SHOTGUNS

CLAIRE HEWITT and her father rode into town early the morning of the trial. Doc and Charlie had disappeared the night before.

They found Longhorn seething. Already at nine o'clock the saloons were doing a land office business! Townspeople, punchers from the neighboring ranches, transient strangers, all talked of little but the trial. The fact that Lance and Flint had killed two men while in the act of rustling cattle made the charge murder as well as theft. A verdict of guilty meant that they would hang. And it had already become apparent that though conviction might come through legal means, the execution might easily be illegal—and immediate.

Hewitt left Claire at the hotel while he circulated among the saloons and the groups congregated along the main street. But he cut short his investigation when it became apparent that not everybody would be able to crowd into the courtroom. He picked up Claire and together they joined the group outside the frame building where the trials were to be held. Doc and Charlie were there and Hewitt and Claire joined them. Immediately they were the subject of curious glances.

It was known that Doc and Charlie were friends of the accused men and it was suspected that they had been partners in the rustling. There had even been hints in the saloon talk that they might be strung up with the others. The fact that they worked now for Hewitt marked him and Claire for special attention and was perhaps the strongest point in Lance's and Flint's favor.

Presently the sheriff came down the street at the head of four deputies, between whom marched the prisoners, handcuffed. Sheriff Baker looked grim. He knew as well as anyone the temper of the crowd, and he was anxious not to have his record spoiled by having his prisoners taken away from him. The march down the street to the courtroom had been, in fact, especially staged, for the sheriff intended that the crowd should believe

Beside Doc stood Charlie Parr, white mustache bristling, blue
eyes blazing coldly over the twin barrels of his shotgun.

that they would be marched back that way after the trial. That would make it easier to return them to the jail by a back way.

The group at the door of the courtroom separated to let them through. It was noticeable that Doc and Charlie stood well back on the edge of the group, contenting themselves merely with nodding cheerfully to Lance and Flint. Immediately the door was opened the crowd started to surge through. It was then that Sheriff Baker pulled his first surprise of the day. Two deputies standing at the door fanned and disarmed everyone who came in.

Hewitt groaned inwardly; Claire paled. Doc and Charlie had been among the first to enter and so among the first to have their guns collected. Having gotten that far they had no chance to back out. They had to submit and go in. And the deputies fanned them thoroughly. Not even a sleeve derringer could have escaped that search.

The court room was a high-ceilinged room, lighted, not very adequately, by three windows set high in the walls. The windows were too high for anyone standing on the ground to look through. There was a back door, locked and guarded, for Baker, in addition to the four deputies who had escorted the prisoners had strung a cordon around the building. Most of these men were in front but two of them were in the rear, with instructions to watch the door and to keep everyone away from the windows.

The preliminaries of the trial were gotten through in short order and the trial itself did not drag much. After the jury was sworn in, the town marshal, in the rôle of prosecutor, got up and stated his case briefly.

"These here prisoners," he summed up finally, "have got a story, which cain't be disproved but cain't be proved, neither. The only chance they got of provin' where they got the cattle at all, would be to go down into Mexico an' git the feller they say they rustled 'em from. Nobody tried that, because it stands to reason that the Mex, if such a feller actually exists, ain't goin' to come over here an' admit he's been buying wet cattle. Which anyway, he wouldn't have no love for the hombres that stole 'em from him, an' wouldn't do it even if he wasn't scared to. But all that there is only admittin' the prisoners ain't lyin'. The way it stands now, it's their word ag'in the word of a prominent citizen of this here city. An' we've shore got to a pretty state of things if we're goin' to take the word of wide-loopers and killers ag'in a hombre like him. I'm goin' to call him to the stand right now, him and then his foreman, Jake Levitt, an' after that I'm shore a-goin' to ask you to bring a verdict that'll hang these gun-slingers plenty high."

TESTIMONY WAS brief. Lowery told his story and was corroborated by Levitt. Then Lance repeated his side of the affair and Flint told the same story. No mention was made of young Hewitt. Although his father had felt in honor bound to urge it Doc and Charlie had vetoed the suggestion. The boy, they thought privately, was probably dead. And if he were not, Ogalally would have him killed at the first suggestion that he might be called to testify.

As a lawyer for their friends, Doc and Charlie had engaged the town's best—a gentleman called Wagon Grease Kelleher, who made a vague living out of intermittent cases. He had won his nickname because some wag had suggested that no one could work his drinking elbow so easy and frequent unless he oiled it with something. Wagon Grease was noted for his eloquence, especially when properly primed with red-eye. Now he made a flaming speech in favor of the defendants, dwelling particularly on Lowery's too-providential appearance with his army at so unlikely a spot. After that the jury retired to deliberate.

Claire's heart sank. She felt that they were trapped here in this well-like room, with its high, guarded windows and its locked doors before each of which stood an armed deputy. Doc and Charlie were helpless; the verdict was sure. For the dozenth time she sought Lance's eyes to convey to him her friendship and sympathy. She tried not to look discouraged, but despite her best efforts her lips quivered.

She could see Doc and Charlie sitting on one of the front benches, but could not see their expressions. Then the jury filed in, and the foreman rose to deliver their verdict.

"Your honor," he said deliberately, "this here jury finds this kind of a funny case—which it wouldn't be too much to say there's a strong smell of skunk somewhere's about it"—here he looked meaningly at Lowery. "On the other hand," he went on, "these here prisoners was caught with the goods, so to speak. If their intentions was innocent, like they say, they was shore unfortunate. Consequent, this jury finds that they had the hard luck to be guilty and recommends that they git a rope collar prompt an' sudden, which when they're plenty dead, they ain't apt to rustle much cows."

He sat down grimly, amid a sudden roar of approval from the audience. Claire's heart began to beat painfully. She recognized the menace in that growl of applause. About her everywhere, men were getting their feet.

"Set down, set down!" the judge shouted angrily. "This here court ain't dismissed yet."

In the confusion Claire did not see Doc and Charlie bend over and reach under the long wooden bench on which they sat. She only saw them come up, each with sawed-off shotgun in his hand, as though the weapons had materialized out of thin air!

"Keep your hand away from that gun, Baker," Doc Grimson's voice snarled like a sudden trumpet. "The first man who makes a misplay'll get himself blown to hell!"

The courtroom froze. Danger sat in the man's voice and manner like a living presence. Beside him stood Charlie Parr, almost as formidable, white-mustache bristling with determination, blue eyes a-blaze. In the hands of those two, the shotgun barrels looked like the yawning eye-sockets of death itself.

"Get your hands up!" Doc's voice crackled. "All you deputies and Baker."

Nobody hesitated. The hands went up as though jerked by the same string. As though it were a signal, Charlie Parr leapt toward the rear window, placed a chair under it and leaned out, the gun before him. "Reach!" he barked to the outside guards.

The handcuffs had been taken off Lance and Flint after they had gotten to the courtroom. As Charlie leapt for the window they moved just as fast toward the sheriff and his guns. Claire felt sure they hadn't been warned beforehand. But the team-play was perfect.

"The key to the back door is in that guard's pocket, Lance," Doc snapped. "Get it!" A second later the door was open, and the guards were under Lance's gun. Charlie Parr came down from the window. The door slammed behind all four. The whole play had not taken twenty seconds.

Sheriff Baker cursed and dashed for the door. His deputies crowded after him. A yell from the guards in the rear brought the crowd running from the front of the building. A shot rang out. Another; then a sharp fusillade. Claire heard the rapid drum of hoofs. Yells, and more shots.

A voice shouted a curse. "They've made it! Get your horses, boys, quick!"

HEWITT LED Claire out of the courtroom. He could scarcely keep the jubilation out of his voice, "Slickest thing I ever saw!" he exclaimed in an enthusiastic whisper. "After that I'll believe they can get away with anything!" He need scarcely have troubled to keep his voice down, for the street was swarming with noise and confusion as the posse formed. Nor was Hewitt alone in his admiration. Men who would have hanged all four or shot them at sight were almost equally enthusiastic.

"Never saw the beat of it!"

"Danged if I don't hope they'll get away!"

"They must have slipped in last night and rigged them benches up to hold the shot guns. Neatest trick I ever see…. Baker'll never get 'em with those horses!"

The sheriff and his posse, however, were nearer to catching

up with them than the enthusiasts believed. Once it was understood what had happened, it was only a matter of seconds for men to get to their mounts, which were tied up at the town's various hitching racks, and to take the trail. The vanguard of the pursuit was not two minutes behind the four as it left town. Across the level country a full-voiced shout went up at the sight of them, and the possemen fed steel to their mounts in an effort to make a short chase of it.

Not that that was easy to do. No four men in the countryside were better able to rate horses than these men outside the law. And they were all well mounted. Doc and Charlie had seen to that.

Lance, turning in his saddle and seeing the pursuit, grinned and yelled across to Charlie Parr: "Looks like a parade."

Charlie nodded, his eyes twinkling. "We'll set 'em a little problem before long," he called back.

They were pounding toward broken country and Lance knew that when Charlie set out to blind the trail those who followed were apt to find themselves in trouble.

Over the top of a sharp rise Charlie swung quickly to the left and the others followed. Ahead of them a network of arroyos opened, cut into the sandy soil between formations of red, crumbling rock. Into them the old outlaw plunged, followed in single file by the others. For the next fifteen minutes they rode a twisting maze, out of one arroyo and into another, following every path where rock offered an opportunity to conceal their sign.

Presently, they struck a shallow creek and followed it downstream, though their course should have been in the opposite direction. Lance wondered, but understood when Charlie left the stream at the entrance of an arroyo which twisted a course in the upstream direction. Nevertheless, as Charlie still followed a twisted course angling always to the left and south, Lance began to doubt again. At the first sign that they had taken to the arroyos, he felt certain the posse would split. Then, while a portion would attempt to follow their trail, others would ride hard, circling, to try and cut them off.

Their natural course was toward the hills and the badlands beyond, and it seemed to him that they were taking the longest way to get there. If any of their pursuers were wise enough to ride straight they might easily get between them and the hills. And there were some good sign-hunters riding with the posse. Men with grimly-set, determined jaws and ready rifles jutting from saddle boots....

CHAPTER 14
RIDERS OF THE NIGHT

THE ARROYO they were following ended on the side of a rocky slope. They picked their way carefully, keeping to the rocks, and then raced down the opposite slope, and out into the open country again.

As they hit the flat land, Lance saw the wisdom of Charlie's course. They were in reality on a short cut to the southern hills which led down into Mexico. Over that broken country he could not have come much straighter to his objective, and he had put some high, difficult country between them and the posse. Any dust they raised would not be seen from a distance. The only way to follow them was to follow the sign they had necessarily left, for in that country the arroyos might have led off in any direction. And it would take time to decipher the sign they had made. They must have gained at least half an hour, perhaps an hour or more.

After another fifteen minutes riding they crossed another rise and Charlie pulled up. "Here we are," he said cheerfully to Doc.

Doc Grimson nodded and turned to the others. Briefly, he told them what he had heard at Lowery's the night before and his and Charlie's promise to Hewitt.

"Charlie thinks he can throw 'em off the trail here for good," he ended, "and we can hide out in the broken brush country the other side of these sand dunes until night. Then we can drift down to Hewitt's. What do you say—want to sit in?"

Flint gave him one of his melancholy smiles. "Kind of," he said.

"Do we want to sit in?" Lance crowed. "Say, I'd ride down from here to Canada on a burro to stick cactus in that Lowery's pants."

Doc nodded. "Tell 'em your idea, Charlie."

"Well," Charlie said, "She's simple but she ought to work slick as bear's grease. This mornin' early I hazed a good sized bunch of Hewitt's fuzz-tails over here to the sand dunes—crossed the sand with 'em twice and let 'em graze all around the edges so that it's well tracked up. Then I pushed 'em gentle around the rim of the bad country and left 'em loose there on Hewitt's range. Most of 'em are likely still there. What we'll do is this: we'll lift the shoes off our horses. The sand won't hold the tracks much or show how fresh they are. We'll pile our packs on one of 'em and lead him over to where the rocks begin. From there we can carry the leather on foot without leavin' any sign, to a hideout I've got picked. Then we'll ride the broncs slow, lettin' 'em graze, over the trail I left this mornin' and turn 'em loose near the others. We can dismount on the rocks, so as to leave no sign.

"These fellers behind us will be lookin' for *shod* horses, four of 'em together and goin' fast. This sand leads right up to the rocky country where a trail will take some lookin' for anyway. They'll conclude that we passed over it, hit the rocks and are on our way through the hills to Mexico. There ain't no place in that brush up there where four horses can be hid, and they just naturally won't think of lookin' for us there. We'll rub down our mounts before we send 'em a-rackin' down to join the others. At a distance, they'll look all right. You know a feller sees mostly what he's lookin' for, anyway. An' that bunch'll be in a hurry. They won't stop to think."

"Of course," Doc said curtly, "it's a chance to take. If it doesn't work, we'll be caught a-foot and have to fight it out."

"Yeah," Charlie agreed drily, "an' there's enough of those fellers to fill us so full of lead we won't even have to be buried—we'll just naturally sink."

"On the other hand," Doc pointed out, "The trail into Mexico

A yell from Lance brought Doc to the window. Two riders had broken through

the advancing line of gunmen and were making for the house at a dead run.

is clear and straight, if we want to take it. They'll never catch up with us."

"Let's get to work," Flint Maddox said, his eyes beginning to glow in a way which curiously lifted the sadness from his big-featured face.

Lance grinned. "Flint said it!" he agreed. "Let's go!"

Charlie said placidly: "There ain't any hurry. It ought to take that posse an hour to unravel our trail. I'll just ride up to the ridge and take a look-see, then we'll go ahead."

HE BACK-TRAILED to the top of the rise and when he

came back, much of his calm had vanished. His face was working with a mixture of excitement, disappointment and incredulity.

"Dang me," he exclaimed, "if they ain't comin' already!"

Lance swore. "How close?" he asked.

"Big dust cloud at the edge of that last arroyo," Charlie told him, obviously still struggling with his amazement. "About fifteen minutes fast ride off."

"Have we still got time to work it?" Flint asked quickly.

Charlie shook his head. "I don't know," he said slowly. "It'd be closer'n a sidewinder to his skin. You see, we got to separate and graze these horses around out of sight. If a trail looks fresh and straight, they're goin' to follow it and get on to us. I was countin' heavy on their not foolin' with the trail of a grazin' horse."

Doc said reluctantly: "I'm afraid it would be a fool chance to take, now that they're so close."

"What about high-tailin' it into the mountains, losin' 'em and then ridin' back?" Flint suggested.

"There ain't but a couple of trails," Doc said, "and they'd split to cover those. If we let 'em keep driving us until dark, we won't get back in time."

"The worst of it is," Charlie groaned. "They've got some jasper with that posse who can read sign plenty!"

"Listen," Lance said swiftly. "We can't go off and leave that old man and his daughter without any help. Here's what we'll do. I'll stay up at the top of the rise and shoot enough to hold 'em up. That'll give you fellows time to work your stunt. Then I'll let 'em chase me into the hills. They'll naturally figure you're ahead of me. I'll ride back as soon as I can, but if I'm not there in time, you hombres will be."

"Nothin' doing," said Doc positively. "It's all of us or none of us."

"Doc's right," Charlie agreed. "You'd be practically beggin' for soogans in Boot Hill."

"Then let's all chance it," said Lance impetuously.

"I'm willin'," Flint Maddox said, his mouth tight. "We can always notch off some of 'em before they plant us. I never did like bein' chased myself."

Doc and Charlie looked at one another, grim-faced. "We sat in," Charlie said. "I never did like to throw in my hand to a skunk."

"Neither do I," Doc said smiling thinly. "Let's play it to a finish."

Hurriedly they moved into the center of the dunes and set about unshoeing their mounts. They worked swiftly and in silence, conscious that the menace of the dust-cloud moving across the level behind them grew with every second.

"Now separate," Charlie directed when the job was done, "and work toward the edge. When you get there, let 'em graze. Once we get out of sight around that rim of brush and rocks we can unsaddle and turn the broncs loose. Don't hurry it—it's got to look natural."

The minutes which followed were perhaps the most tense which even these men had experienced. To fight is one thing; to wait to fight is another and worse; but to race a grazing horse against sudden death from behind—that needs nerve!

Lance saw that Charlie Parr had chosen the longest route for himself. Doc Grimson was next, then Lance, then Flint. Deliberately Lance chose a more circuitous course, working farther out, so that, he and Charlie would reach cover at about the same moment.

He thought to himself that they must make a funny sight—four men, fanned out under the hammering sun, grazing their horses, a hundred yards or more apart. And always behind them that dust cloud must be growing larger, nearer. His back felt cold under the brazen hammers of the sun. His horse, tired, moved with maddening deliberation. He tried to calculate how much time lay between him and cover but estimating the erratic course of a feeding animal was too difficult.

He glanced at the others. They sat slouched easily in their saddles, in appearance totally unconcerned. What were they feeling? He, too, was riding easily, but the sweat on his forehead was no less icy for that.

HOW MUCH time had gone by? Seven minutes? Ten? He thought that he had moved far enough outward and kneed his horse gently to head him toward the edge of the broken country. Now at least he was grazing toward cover. Crop and move forward. Crop and zigzag. Don't interfere too much. It's got to look natural.

Was it his imagination or did he hear something? His mount flung up his head, looking backward, his ears pointed. Yes, there it was again. A low steady rumble almost inaudible, like a muffled beating within the air. The thud of half a hundred hoofs out on the plain behind.

His nerves suddenly began an intolerable itching and jumping under his skin. He still had a long way to go. Couldn't they put the horses at least into a walk now? Stray animals might stop grazing and start walking or even trotting at any time for any reason. Nobody would follow the trail of a stray this far, anyway. At this rate they wouldn't make it. And that low thunder was getting clearer now every second!

Damn the fool bronc! He was going slower now. Every few seconds he stopped grazing and lifted his head to listen. Lance looked at Doc who shot him a sudden, brilliant smile. He grinned back, his heart suddenly warming. He might be shot in the back, but at least he'd go out with real men.

Behind the ridge the hoof-thunder was a rising crescendo. He heard voices shouting. Any second now they'd burst over the rise all spread out—and that would be the finish.

His horse stopped and whirled, facing the noise. Was the fool going back to investigate it? Lance prepared to knee him around again. But the pony turned back on his own initiative and began to trot toward the edge of the brush! He had taken alarm, as any stray would have. The other ponies were infected with the same idea. Flint was around the turn, now, hidden from the ridge. Doc next. Now himself and Charlie. He looked back. They must be coming up the slope. And then he was around, the ridge hidden from him. His heart came down out of his throat and he felt the warm color of restored circulation flood up into his face.

Charlie, just ahead of him, turned in the saddle. "Quick now!"

he said in a low voice, "we've got to get the broncs away while they're still makin' plenty of noise."

In single file they rode up by the side of a tumbled mass of rocks, dismounted on them, and dragged the saddles from the horses' backs.

From where they were now the land sloped away into a grassy basin and Lance saw twenty or thirty broomtails grazing there. Hurriedly Lance swabbed at his mount's saddle sweat and sent him with a sharp flick of his rope down to join the others. Then cautiously he followed Charlie and the rest up the rocks into the brush. Ten minutes in the sun would dry that sweat so it would not be noticeable from a distance.

But would they have ten minutes? Already the steady beat of hoofs had stopped and he could hear voices shouting directions. The posse had come to the sand dunes and must be circling them now for sign.

Three minutes crawling brought them to a wide crack in the rocks which narrowed down to a narrow aperture at one end. A man of Lance's size had to squeeze himself pretty tight to get through that opening, but once through, and dragging his saddle after him, he found himself in a small cave, not more than ten by ten, but dry and comfortable. They'd be safe there— so long as nobody found them. But once found they'd be trapped like rats in a hole.

"We can slip out now and take a look," Charlie said calmly. "The rim of the crack is brushy. But be plenty careful. If they ever see us we'll have about as much chance as four scorpions in a bottle."

From their position in the fissure it was possible to overlook the basin where the horses grazed but not the sand dunes. They could hear scattered and confused talk from there but could not make out anything that was said. Evidently the posse was at a loss. Presently, however, a figure in buckskin pants and big black sombrero came around the edge of the brush, leading his horse and bending over the tracks left by their horses.

"Ah-h," Charlie breathed softly.

Lance knew what he meant without explanation. He guessed that the figure below them was a half-breed—an Apache, probably. Undoubtedly he was the one who, as Charlie had said, could "read sign plenty."

AS THEY looked the tracker lifted his head and saw the horses grazing below him. The sight stopped him. Lance held his breath. Would he go on or turn back? On the rocks twenty yards ahead of him would be infinitesimal traces—little scraped places made by their boots.

The expression on the man's face was not visible but the very attitude of his body showed bewilderment and indecision. Lance could imagine his mental processes. He had followed the traces of grazing horses merely because they were the only fresh tracks to be seen. But he must have followed them without any real conviction. It would be hard to believe that fugitives, hard-pressed by the law, would have let their mounts feed in the long and leisurely fashion which the tracks and freshly cropped grass must have shown him. And now before his eyes were the horses, probably, which had made the tracks.

After a moment an idea seemed to occur to him and he

mounted and rode toward the loose broncs. Lance footed at Doc and Charlie. Charlie's face was grim, his eyes narrowed, following the riding figure. Doc's gray eyes returned his gaze with cool humor. "It's always the unexpected that happens," he remarked smiling. "Who'd have thought they'd have an Indian tracker? The question now is whether to make a fight of it here in the open or crawl back in that hole on the slim chance he'll overlook us. Once in there we can't even sell out with guns."

Charlie growled, "Once he starts up these rocks we're done for. Sign a white man couldn't see'll lead him to us quicker'n hell can scorch a feather."

But instead of riding straight for the horses the half-breed swung out in a wide circle around the basin.

"Thinks maybe we changed broncs here," Charlie chuckled, "and is cuttin' for sign to see where we broke out."

Flint said: "I've got a hunch he won't get on to us. If he's a 'Pache he won't be able to even imagine that four men left their horses without getting any new ones. The last thing a 'Pache lets loose of is his pony."

They watched the mounted figure make his circle, noting that by good luck the horses they had just turned loose were toward the center of it, their sweat marks already invisible except to close inspection. Not finding sign, the 'breed cast what was probably a puzzled glance around the horizon and then turned back toward the dunes.

The four waited. After a few minutes they heard a shout, a voice calling orders, then the renewed sound of many hoofs as the posse moved off, taking a trail which led it through the broken country behind the four. From the sound of posse's progress it had not split up. The group of law men had moved off purposefully, steadily, and all together, as though it had picked up the trail again.

The men in the fissure exchanged questioning glances. "Now what?" growled Charlie suspiciously. The thing smelled like a trap.

It was to Doc Grimson that the real explanation first came. He shook suddenly with silent laughter.

"It's always the unexpected that happens," he exclaimed softly. "Who'd have thought our lives would hang on a 'breed's vanity? He couldn't find a trail, so, by God, he *invented* one!"

CHAPTER 15
BOOT HILL BOUND!

TWO HOURS after nightfall there were two light taps, then two more, on the rear window of the Hewitt living room. Hewitt rose hastily, and Claire with him, her eyes shining. It was the signal agreed upon with Doc Grimson and Charlie Parr.

"Put out the light, daughter," Hewitt directed, and went to the window. Doc Grimson was there, and by his side Claire could see Lance Clayton. Behind were the dim figures of Charlie and Flint Maddox.

Claire reached out an eager hand to Doc and then, blushing a little in the darkness, to Lance. "I'm so glad," she whispered.

Lance squeezed her hand. "Not any gladder than we are," he said softly.

"Sheriff Baker's been here," Hewitt cautioned them. "And he may come back. But I reckon it's safe for you to come in an' get some grub. Claire's got everything about ready, waitin' for you."

"You sound like you expected us," Charlie Parr twinkled at him when they had come inside and the shutters had been closed.

Hewitt chuckled. "Baker got here just about an hour ago," he explained. "Mad and plenty suspicious. Seems like they had a breed tracker with 'em who lost your trail. Lost it first at the sand hills and then seemed to pick it up again for some hours until he lost it again up in the hills. I gathered that Baker thought he'd really lost it the first time and was bluffin' after that. The 'breed ain't one of your friends, is he?"

"Without knowing it, he's just that," Doc Grimson smiled. "Funny how these famous trackers would rather do anything than admit they've lost a trail."

"Anyway," Hewitt went on, "Baker figured those sand hills was too near my range to make me innocent. I wouldn't wonder if I'd better stand guard outside while you eat. He might be back. Claire'll take care of you, and when you're fed you can bed down in the hayloft."

The four sat down to a supper of big juicy steaks, eggs, potatoes and fluffy biscuits, and sighed happily. They had walked seven miles since nightfall, carrying forty-pound saddles, and they were tired and hungry men.

"Tell me," Claire asked when the edge of their appetites had been worn down a little, "what's going to happen in the morning."

Doc Grimson smiled at her. "You tell us," he said.

Charlie Parr's eyes sparkled under his bushy white eyebrows. "You ever hear about the man that went rattlesnake huntin' and got a skunk by the tail?" he inquired. "When a feller goes huntin' before daybreak, there ain't no tellin' what he'll run into."

"Anyway," Lance said, grinning, "whatever it is, it ain't goin' to keep me away from breakfast—not if you're goin' to make some more of these biscuits, it ain't!"

"Be serious!" Claire said. "I want to know. Isn't Ogalally likely to have more men than you are? And what do you think they're going to try to do?"

"That's what we've got to find out, Claire," Doc told her quietly. Maybe they're going to try to run off some of your cattle again. If they are, Ogalally may not bring all his gang. Maybe it's something else—maybe only Lowery and Ogalally will be there. We've got to see."

Before dawn next morning, with little certainty of what lay before them, the five men moved out in the darkness. They took their position on the rim of an arroyo less than fifty yards from the water hole at which Lowery and Ogalally were to meet.

It was well that they had gotten an early start for they had not been there more than fifteen minutes when they heard hoof-beats of a group of riders. The light was still too dim to make out their identity or numbers. But what was more than clear to everybody was that there were too many of them. A good two dozen, Doc estimated. Evidently Ogalally had brought the whole gang, and Lowery his own gunmen. It looked bad.

There was the sound of wire-cutters, and then the group moved onto Flying M Bar land.

Lowery's voice, heavy and commanding rang out: "Spread out and round up the cattle boys. Take your time. There'll be nobody to see you except Hewitt, and he won't be able to talk. Remember, it's five hundred extra to the man that cuts him down!"

DOC WHISTLED softly under his breath. Lowery was running a higher blaze than he had thought. He must feel pretty safe and pretty sure of the men he had under him. If any of those gun-slingers ever got sore and talked…! But Doc had encountered such over-confident hombres before. They never believed anyone would have the nerve to betray them—not *them!* Lowery apparently had plans of empire, and believed nothing could stop him.

Doc had hoped to drive the marauders off easily, capturing one or two of them in the hope that they would talk and convict the crooked ranchman, but this was a different matter. His own impulse was as always to drive ahead and let the danger take care of itself. But the responsibility of leadership was on him. If he tried to break up this play now, he'd be more than likely to sacrifice the lives of his partners as well as his own. The sensible thing to do was to let them go ahead and take their trail while Hewitt rode for the sheriff.

The decision was taken out of his hands by Lowery himself.

"Levitt," he called, "Take five of our men and surround the ranch house. See that the girl doesn't get away."

"She won't," the foreman replied jeeringly. "An' remember, I'm to be the parson at the weddin'."

There was a laugh from the group and Lowery said, with a note of self-satisfaction in his voice. "I'm not aimin' to marry her. Somebody else can do that, after I've had enough of her."

Hewitt cursed aloud, his voice thick with fury. "Damn you, I'll kill you for that." As he spoke he half-raised himself into view.

There was a sharp exclamation from the group and a Winchester belched flame in the semi-darkness. The bullet smacked the dust several inches from Hewitt's shoulder. The answer was a volley of rifle fire which emptied a couple of saddles and threw the mounted group into confusion. Taken by surprise they scattered at a gallop.

Lance cursed between his teeth, steadily, monotonously.

"Steady, son," Charlie advised him quietly.

"I missed that skunk, Lowery," Lance swore.

"You'll have another chance at him," Doc said grimly. "They haven't gone far." Hewitt's had been a fool play, but he was glad somehow, that it had happened that way.

"Yeah," commented Charlie Parr dryly, "an' you're goin' to have plenty of daylight to see him by."

Even as he spoke the eastern sky was lightening rapidly. The dawn mists lifted; a low, small cloud turned pink. A shaft of scarlet shot upward, fanned out into a many-colored flame. The

115

swift, stupendous dawn of the southern Borderlands was on them.

As the light grew they were able to see that the outlaws with their horses had disappeared completely.

"Cached their broncs in the bottom yonder by them cotton-woods, I bet," Charlie hazarded. "They'll be crawlin' out behind that there brush."

A movement behind a clump of mesquite about two hundred yards to the front caught his eye. He sighted and fired. The mesquite gave a convulsive jerk and then was still.

"Winged him anyway," Charlie announced grimly. The words weren't out of his mouth before a hot rifle fire from the brush began. Lead sung around the outlaw in an angry swarm. One of the bullets lifted the hat from his head.

"Them fellers kin shoot better'n I give 'em credit for," he muttered, unmoved. The outlaws had picked good cover and the only targets were the occasional movement of an arm and the white puffs of smoke from the rifles.

"Take it easy, boys," Doc Grimson warned. "One slow hit is worth three fast misses."

The admonition was hardly necessary, unless for Hewitt. Lance, Charlie and Flint were taking their time.

LANCE WAS drawing a bead on a red-flannelled elbow, He had fired once into the brush beside it, without result, so he had decided to choose the target he could see. He squeezed the trigger. The elbow jumped sharply and pulled out of sight. A man opposite Doc Grimson stood up suddenly behind his bush and fell forward into it.

As Doc levered to fire again he felt a sharp tug at his sleeve. He looked down in time to see a second bullet kick up a puff of dust from the bank below him. Some of Ogalally's gang had worked around and were firing from the low hill behind them.

"Drop down, boys!" Doc called sharply. "It's time to move back."

The others obeyed promptly. They also had become aware of the firing behind them. Lance had had his shoulder creased; it streamed blood, but Doc's first glance at the wound told him that it was nothing to be feared.

Keeping to the arroyo, they worked their way back toward the ranch-house. They divided up, two on each side, with Lance, to his disgust, leading the horses, and fell back by relays. One man on each side would go up the bank and fire a few shots to keep the outlaws from following too fast, while the others went along fifteen or twenty yards and did the same thing.

Ogalally's gang and the Lazy L crowd closed in behind them, but they moved slowly, dodging from cover to cover.

So slow was their progress that the four had time to put their horses in the barn and gain the ranch-house without risk. Flint was left behind in the barn loft, to pick off anybody who attempted to sneak up and set the place on fire.

Claire greeted them, white-faced but quiet, with a rifle in her hand. She had heard the firing and had closed all the shutters in the house. "I had just begun to think I'd ride out to you," she told them.

"You get in a corner and keep out of the way of stray lead, daughter," Hewitt told her.

117

"No. I can shoot and I'm going to take my place with the rest."

"No—please!" Lance cut in imperatively. "This is no job for a girl."

"We'll all feel better if you stay out of the way, honey," Charlie Parr told her gently.

There was a burst of firing from outside and lead ripped through the door and window shutters.

"How many of those men are there?" Claire asked.

"Not enough to hurt," Doc Grimson lied. "We'll call on you if we need you, Claire."

Not enough to hurt! No, not enough to do more than cut them down one by one until the house was silent and Lowery could come and snatch a frantic girl from over the broken body of her father. Doc Grimson foresaw, as the rest did, how the fight must go. Hemmed in, out-numbered five to one, there was no chance for them unless help came. And help couldn't come. Anyone else who showed up would just swell the forces against them when they heard that Lowery was trying to capture four escaped rustlers. But they would be cut down, probably, long before anyone came at all. Good shooting might cut down the odds a little, but not enough.

The house was not a good place to defend. The adobe walls were bullet-proof but the doors and shutters were not. It was necessary to shoot from peep-holes in the windows, and the attackers would be wise enough to concentrate their fire on these spots. It would have been far better to have kept up a running fight in the open, but the presence of Claire had made that impossible.

"How many windows are there altogether?" Doc asked.

"Four in the front, two in the back, two on one side and one on the other," Hewitt counted. "That makes nine."

"We'll each take two then," Doc said. "Shoot a while from one of your windows, then move to the other. If you keep picking the window they're not shooting at, we can do a lot of damage before they nick any of us. Remember that every time you shoot you draw their fire, so when you do shoot, *hit* something!"

THEY TOOK positions, Doc and Charlie in front, Lance and Hewitt at each side. Back of the house was a wide stretch without any cover at all. Flint, from the loft of the barn, would be able to keep anyone from crossing there. Charlie Parr crawled carefully to his windows and opened the shutters. Doc did likewise. Lance watched them a minute thoughtfully, then he did the same thing.

"Go tell your dad he better open his, Claire," Charlie advised. "Them loopholes give a good target to shoot at, and when the shutters ain't bullet-proof all they do is to group the other fellow's shot just where they'll do the most good."

For a few minutes it was hot work. Such a hail of lead swept through the windows that it was almost impossible to sight and fire. But the enemy fire slackened after its first frenzied burst and Doc and Charlie began to get in their deadly, accurate work.

Claire, going to take Charlie's advice to her father, had found him with comparatively little to do. The best cover was in front of the house and the attackers had apparently concentrated their forces there. She returned to the long living room with its four windows opening on the front and one to the side.

Here, Doc, Charlie and Lance were at work. It was a sight that brought sudden color to the girl's pale cheeks. Old Charlie, who had seemed to her so gentle, twinkling his garrulous humor throughout the days just past, looked like a Viking, his old eye's blazing, his weathered wrinkled fate, with its fierce white mustache, intent and grim as the death he dealt.

Doc Grimson's hawk-nosed face looked merely absorbed, like that of a scientist lost in some remote laboratory problem. Only the intensified glow in his fine eyes gave a hint that he found the problem exciting! They looked immensely luminous, those eyes, and full of some far, strange pleasure.

Lance was otherwise. A kind of insanely joyous vitality seemed to blaze out from him. It brought his features alive with the most brilliant vitality Claire had ever seen. It was instinct in his posture; glowed from the very movement of his hands as he levered his Winchester. He looked to Claire like some young exultant god of battle, glorying in the hot smoke and flame of battle.

The sight of the three humbled her, somehow. Not many women were privileged to look on brave men at the hour of trial. Strange, she thought suddenly, fighting is a terrible thing, yet fighting men are splendid.

But the sight of Lance saddened her a little while it made her heart beat faster. Here was no good husband and father—not yet, anyhow! Here was someone made for battle, danger, and the risks more cautious and less able men feared to take. Instinctively, she knew that if he were caught in the four pleasant walls of a home he would be as much the caged hawk he had been in prison.

As she looked and thought this, there was a sudden exclamation from Charlie Parr. On the slope before the house, just out of rifle range, a figure had ridden into view. At that distance it was hard to tell, but it looked like Sheriff Baker.

At Charlie's warning glance, Doc Grimson got his marine glass and peered through it. When he turned back toward the room his face was full of ironical amusement. "Enter, the Law," he announced simply.

Another figure went dodging back through the brush and came out on the slope. Red Ed Lowery.

"Looks like that sheriff keeps interruptin' Red just when he's doin' justice," Lance said, grinning.

"This time," Charlie remarked grimly, "it won't be an interruption. It'll be one more rifle for the other side."

"If he's brought his posse, or rides for help, this party's goin' to get right amusin'," Lance said.

Doc Grimson smiled to himself secretly. A few more odds couldn't make much difference in the end, and he knew Lance knew it. He said, "Go get your father, Claire."

The firing had slackened somewhat at the appearance of the sheriff, and now, as the two men on the slope conferred, it almost stopped.

"Look here, Hewitt," Doc said pleasantly. "We're in a kind of a bad place. We can't give up. I reckon you know we'd be strung up five minutes after that gang got hold of us. But there's no use of your staying here. You've got Claire to think of. Now that Baker's here, Lowery may be afraid to try anything against you and Claire. We'll give him a white flag and you two can go out."

Hewitt hesitated. It was easy to see that he was torn between loyalty to the men who had risked everything to help him and his anxiety about his daughter. In the end he found a way to serve both.

"Claire'll go," he said quietly. "Baker'll take care of her. I'm stayin'."

Claire's face flushed indignantly. "Do you think I'm a coward and a quitter, just because I'm a woman?" she demanded passionately. "I won't go a step—do you hear?—until Baker sees to it that Lance and Doc and Charlie and Flint get a chance to go free."

And from that position nothing could move her.

"Look here then," Doc said finally. "Why not let Claire go out and talk to Baker. She can tell him what happened here this morning—how Lowery was tryin' to run off your stock. From what you say, Baker's honest. Maybe he'll be able to call off the dogs. If he's got a posse with him, he'll be able to."

"I'll go out and tell him," Hewitt declared, his jaw setting.

"No," Charlie objected. "It's too much risk, Hewitt. Some of those jaspers'll crack down on you, white flag or no white flag, to get that five hundred Lowery offered. Nobody'd be able to tell which one of 'em done it. They won't shoot at Claire."

Without waiting for further discussion, the girl darted into a bed room and returned with a pillow case, which she waved out the window. Then she opened the door and stepped out.

CHAPTER 16
GUNMEN—AND A GIRL

SHERIFF BAKER, when he got back to Longhorn the night before, had become more and more suspicious of the way the trail had been lost in the sand dunes, and of those apparently innocent tracks of grazing horses. He determined to set out that morning alone and see if, undisturbed, he might not be able to solve the mystery for himself. The firing from Hewitt's spread had brought him over to investigate.

Lowery, going to meet him on the slope, greeted him grimly.

"You're in time to help take those skunks you let get away, Baker," he said. "Got a posse with you?"

"No," the sheriff told him, "I came alone. How'd you get onto 'em?"

As he denied having a posse with him, Lowery's expression changed. Baker thought he saw satisfaction in his eyes and wondered at it.

"Unlimber your Winchester and come on down and help the boys," the big man told him impatiently.

"Is Hewitt in the house?" the sheriff asked as he dismounted.

"Yep. Looks like he's in cahoots with 'em!"

"Where's Claire?"

"Dunno," Lowery growled. "Let's get action."

123

Sheriff Baker's sense of uneasiness grew. There was something about the ranchman's manner he did not like. "Now that I'm here," he suggested, with an attempt at casualness, "we'd better give 'em another chance to give up. It'll save shootin'!"

Lowery looked at him and laughed brutally. "They ain't had a chance to give up," he said. "And they ain't goin' to git one. Now get this straight, Baker: They won't be taken alive. If they are, we're goin' to hang 'em to the nearest cottonwood. We've had enough monkeyin' with the law. And that goes for Hewitt, too."

The sheriff protested feebly but he was being given orders and he knew it. After all, the first thing to do, he told himself, was to take the rustlers. The question of what was to happen to them afterwards could be settled in due time. Baker was not exactly a sensitive or imaginative man, but there was that in Lowery's manner which told him he had stepped into a dangerous spot. More dangerous than merely the round-up of rustlers. Unless he handled himself properly it might not be a question of keeping his job; it might be a question of hanging on to his life.

And it was as the two turned to rejoin Lowery's men, that they saw the white flag waved from the window of the ranch house and saw Claire step out the door.

Instead of being reassured, Baker's uneasiness increased. He guessed that the people in the house had seen him and were going to ask his protection. And that would mean either refusing to do his duty or having bad trouble with Lowery.

At sight of the girl, Lowery's eyes gleamed, and he set off at a brisk pace to meet her. "Come on," he said triumphantly. "They won't shoot while she's there."

Claire marched straight to Baker. "I want to speak to the sheriff alone," she said resolutely.

Lowery gave an unpleasant laugh. "I reckon the time's come to do our talkin' in the open. The sheriff and I are together," he said, looking significantly at Baker.

"I—I reckon that's right, Claire," the officer agreed, avoiding the girl's eyes. "Say what you've got to say, where everybody can hear it."

As they spoke a number of Lowery's men had closed in around their leader. Ogalally's gang kept their positions at a distance. They were not particularly fond of sheriffs.

Claire paled. She began to wonder for the first time whether the sheriff had come out without a posse, but she had not time to think. She plunged ahead, unaware of the dangerous spot she might be putting the lawman into. To her the Law was a great force; one to be reckoned with at all times. It was not easy for her to think that anyone might be wholly indifferent to it.

"I'm asking for protection against this man," she said, her eyes snapping. "He tried to rustle our cattle this morning and when we caught him at it he tried to kill my father and—and our friends."

LOWERY SHOWED yellow teeth in a contemptuous grin. "Fine story," he said. "You ought to be ashamed of yourself—throwing in with convicted criminals. And your fine father, too. Now I know where my cattle have been goin'."

The girl flared, "I'm not talking to you. Sheriff, we've got five

125

witnesses, and there's a cut fence over there that'll tell the whole story. Look around you—do you know who those men are down there? They're Ogalally Pete's gang—that's who they are! And there's Ogalally with them, on the end. Isn't that proof enough for you that Ed Lowery has been lying all the time when he accused Lance Clayton and Flint Maddox of rustling? The story they told is true. Lowery and Ogalally were working together all the time!"

Sheriff Baker's face drained of color. Following the girl's finger he had seen a silver-conchoed sombrero go down out of sight. The face under it he had not seen, but a certainty was on him that what Claire said was true.

"Not only that," the girl went on, "but my father and the others heard Ed Lowery say that he was going to take me, and that somebody else could marry me when"—she choked suddenly, and the rich color flamed up into her cheeks—"when he got through with me."

Baker could feel Lowery's sardonic, threatening eye on him. About him the circle of gunmen closed in insensibly. From one of the group came a low snicker as the girl finished her sentence.

Cold sweat stood out on the sheriff's forehead. "This—this ain't a very likely story you're tellin', Claire," he stammered. "You—you got to have plenty of proof before you—before you make charges like that against a man."

"Of course it ain't a likely story," Lowery cut in brutally. "This girl's trying to shield convicted murderers and rustlers. It won't work. Get her to the rear, boys. Levitt, you and Ben keep guard over her and see that she don't get loose. Then we'll get on with our business."

"I'm not going to the rear," Claire told him, with more confidence than she felt. "I'm going back to that house. And if the sheriff of this county is an honest man, he'll call off this attack and arrest Ogalally Pete and Ed Lowery!"

"I can't do that, Claire," the sheriff told her, "unless your people give up to the law. They're wanted men."

Lowery's eyes gleamed. "Shore," he said. "That's right. Let 'em give themselves up and then we can parley."

And suddenly that gleam in the ranchman's eyes told Claire all she had to know. Her case had been hopeless from the first. For any of the men in the house to surrender, as long as the sheriff was alone here, would be suicide. She could only hope that Baker would be able to get away, and that once away he would come back with enough honest men to see that justice was dealt. Even then, it seemed all so hopeless, for there was no proof of Lowery's guilt other than her father's word and the words of men wanted by the law—criminals in the eyes of the world.

Ogalally Pete would simply disappear and that would be the end of the evidence against the rancher. Bitter anger burned up in her at the thought. Well, she would go back and die with her men. At least she could do that. Baker was a coward—and even if he had not been, he would probably have been helpless.

"I'm going back now," she said, and turned away.

Lowery leapt toward her and laid a heavy hand on her shoulder. "You ain't goin' anywhere, pretty," he told her harshly.

"From now on, you're goin' with me." The girl swung about, sudden terror in her eyes. "Why—why, you can't keep me," she said, her voice shaking despite herself. "I—I came out under a flag of truce. You—you've got...."

She broke off, reading her answer in the cruelty of the big man's gaze—feeling it in the iron grip on her shoulder.

Desperately, her eyes sought those of the sheriff. His face was white, his eyes nervous. She could read in him that his decent instincts wanted to help her and that his weakness and cowardice urged him to save his own hide.

"You—you better come with me, Claire," he got out. "I reckon I got to put you under arrest for helpin' out criminals."

Lowery turned on him with a snarl. "Keep out of this, Baker," he said, and his tone carried a deadly warning. "*I'm* runnin' this show—not you!"

For a moment Sheriff Baker was silent, his gaze fixed, staring, on the ranchman's face, as though he were looking at the face of death itself. Then he straightened and spoke. His voice was no more than a hoarse croak, but his eyes were suddenly steady.

"You can't harm a girl while I'm here, Lowery," he said. "You'll have to go for your gun and get me first."

The ranchman whirled, let go the girl's shoulders, dropped his hands so that they hung near his guns. "There are half a dozen men here who can beat you to the draw, Baker," he said. "If I don't get you first, one of them will. But you asked for it—you're goin' to get it."

"They won't shoot you, Claire," the sheriff said, without taking his eyes from Lowery. "*Run!*"

As he spoke his hands dived for his guns.

"No!" Claire cried. But she was too late. Baker's gun came up spitting flame, but his bullet went wild. At least four slugs had ripped their way through his body before the hammer of his own Colt fell.

Claire ran then, like a deer.

ONE OF Lowery's men jumped after her and raced toward her, cutting in from an angle. It was a mistaken move. The girl was not between him and the house. Something hit him, hard, just over the heart, and the crack of the rifle never reached his ears. He was dead when his face struck the ground, ploughing up a furrow in the dust. The rest dived for cover.

"Let her go," Lowery yelled "Don't shoot!"

But when the girl had disappeared through the house door the firing began again, more heavily than ever. "That's the last hope then," Hewitt said heavily, after Claire had explained what had happened. "Get under cover, daughter. We'll have to sell out as dear as we can."

The girl took up her rifle. "No," she said resolutely. "I'm going to do my part now. I'd rather be killed than—than—"

She did not finish, and the others were silent. They understood, and in their hearts they agreed.

"Take my place then," Doc said. "I'll slip out and see how Flint's getting along."

Doc Grimson slipped out to the barn and climbed up into the loft. Flint, his customarily melancholy face a-light, grinned at him. He had piled grain sacks in front of him and was shooting through the small window in the rear of the loft. He was untouched.

"It's a tight, Flint," Doc told him cheerfully. "How you making out?"

Flint nodded his head toward the window. "Some of them took a liking to that arroyo. Thought they might sneak up that way. If you look close, you'll see what's left of a couple of 'em."

"Good man! Whittle 'em down!"

Doc went back to the house, to find that Hewitt had been shot through the shoulder. He set to work hurriedly, with Claire's help, to bind the wound.

As his quick, supple fingers patted the bandage in place, a yell from Lance brought him to the window. There had been a sharp burst of firing from one portion of the line. Now two riders had broken through the line in front and were making for the house at a dead run. A hail of bullets cut the ground around them, in front of them and behind them, but for a moment they seemed to bear charmed lives.

"Hot damn!" Lance yelped. "It's Lockjaw!"

Charlie Parr's jaw fell open. "The dang fool!" he marvelled. "The dang ol' hairy son!"

CHAPTER 17
BATTLE!

FOR A moment it looked as though a miracle would actually happen and the two men would make it. But when they were scarcely fifty yards from the house, Lockjaw's horse pitched forward on his neck and turned a complete somersault. Lockjaw sailed over his head, landed with a crash and lay still. The second rider's horse ran a few steps further, squealed, stumbled, and went down in his turn. The rider, however, began rolling awkwardly toward the ranch-house. They observed suddenly that his hands were bound behind him and that he was a Mexican. He looked terrified as he rolled and yelled.

Charlie Parr swore. "It's that Mex, Bautista!"

Lance said: "Stand back from the door. I'm goin' out after Lockjaw."

"The hell you are!" snapped Charlie. "Go git dried behind the ears first. This is a man's job." He snatched the door open and ran out.

Lance flashed after him, his two guns spitting flame and lead with each long-legged stride.

Their appearance was the signal for a heavy burst of firing. They ran on, zigzagging like snipe in flight.

Before they got to him Lockjaw had come to. He staggered to his feet, stood looking wildly about him for a second, and then with a shout dashed for the Mexican, whose frantic rolling had taken him a little off his course. He was headed for the corner of the house instead of for the door.

"Come back, you damn fool!" Charlie Parr roared through the thunder of shots. Then turning to Lance: "Git back inside." And he dashed after Lockjaw. But Lockjaw was not to be stopped any more than a madly stampeding herd of longhorns. He reached the Mexican, put out a hamlike hand to his collar and jerked him to his feet. "The door!" he bellowed. "Vamos, you hunk of crowbait!" And shoving the hapless *haciendero* before him he at last ran for shelter.

Charlie Parr, cursing bitterly, took hold of one of the Mexican's arms and helped to half push, half carry the bleating man out of the rain of rifle fire which hissed, and whined and crackled sudden death about them. Lead tore up the dirt at their feet, ripped through their clothes, smashed against the house ahead of them, but, incredibly, nobody dropped. The two catapulted through the doorway, and the door slammed behind them.

"Hello, Lockjaw," Doc grinned. "Who's your little friend?"

"Him?" Lockjaw answered. "That's Baby." He took Juan Bautista's nose between a large thumb and forefinger and twisted it. "Ain't it, Baby?" he inquired affectionately.

"Looks like you and Baby got tangled up with the same buzz-saw," Charlie Parr said drily, picking up his rifle and turning toward the window.

Lockjaw grinned. "No, not exactly," he said. "Me, I got tangled with Baby's crowd, and then Baby he went an' got hisself tangled with *me*. He didn't feel like talkin'. But he feels like talkin' now—don't you, Baby?" He shoved the Mexican into a corner, with a bellowing laugh.

Both Lockjaw and his captive were lamentable looking objects. Tattered, dust-covered, their faces were cut and bruised almost out of recognition. Of the two, Lockjaw was the worse. His puffed eyes were mere slits. His nose, smashed by the vaquero's gun, wandered over toward his ear. The bullet storm through which he had just passed had been directed largely at him. It had ripped his clothes to shreds. Blood dipped from his bandaged head. The scalp wound which had knocked him out at Don Juan's ranch had been reopened by his fall.

Lance looked at him with amazed delight. "Some man, this Lockjaw," he said, shaking his head and breaking out into uncontrollable, laughter. "Where were you all this time?"

Lockjaw looked sheepish. "They had me tied up, but I broke loose on 'em," he added, grinning.

"There's a extry rifle in the corner, Lockjaw," Charlie Parr said. "Git busy, old son. We ain't got long now before lead-poisonin' sets in."

LOCKJAW SAID "Howdy, ma'am" to Claire, took up the rifle and went to the window. He estimated wind and distance, sighted calmly and squeezed the trigger. One of Lowery's punchers lying under partial cover in a fold in the ground, jerked convulsively and rolled over on his back, gaping at the sky.

"Where's Flint?" he asked, levering and blowing through the open rifle chamber.

"In the barn," Doc told him. "He's got the best of it. The ground out back is clear of cover except for one arroyo so he's holding them back. Most of them are out here in front."

Lockjaw turned to the window and fired again.

"Listen, boys," Hewitt said suddenly. "What do you say we run for it?"

Doc looked at Charlie. "What do you say, amigo?" he asked.

Charlie shook his head. "Why?" he said. "Some of us *might* get through, but they'd be on our tails in two seconds. We got fast horses, but no faster than them of Lowery's. That skunk's got the best horses I ever saw. The country's flat—we wouldn't get away."

"I'd rather not take mine in the back either," Doc said grimly.

"Hell, no!" Lance said. "This way we'll at least get us a passel of them before we check in. An' if we're lucky enough to hold 'em off until dark, whoever's left will stand a chance of getting away. Their fast horses won't count so much then."

Lockjaw had paused in the midst of sighting and had for some seconds been occupied in silent thought. "Them fellers ain't got no horses," he now said, in the tone of one who states a simple fact.

Everyone stared. "What do you mean?" Doc Grimson asked quickly.

"They was a big bunch of 'em back of the ridge right there," Lockjaw explained. "So we run 'em off."

"What in thunder are you talking about?" Charlie Parr shouted. "*Who* run 'em off?"

Lockjaw looked surprised. "Why," he said, "me and the boys."

"What boys, you locoed mudhen?"

Lockjaw looked startled. "Didn't I tell you?" he inquired. "I met up with some of the old boys—the ones you and me used to run with. There was four of them, Featherleg Casey an' Jackpot Jones, an—"

Charlie bellowed, "What happened to 'em, idjit? Where are they now?"

"Why they didn't want to horn in on no play without bein' sure what it was about. So I left 'em yonder back of the ridge and come in to see. They said if you was here and in a tight—"

Lockjaw paused. His jaw dropped open, "Say!" he exclaimed, "I reckon I forgot to signal 'em!"

Charlie Parr was purple in the face. "You mean to tell me—you—you sit there an'—" he choked, bereft of speech.

Lockjaw said: "Aw, Charlie—you told me to pick up the Winchester an' go to work. I—I didn't have time to think!"

Lance fought to keep from laughing again. He had too much love for Lockjaw to want to hurt his feelings, but it was pretty hard not to, sometimes.

"They said to wave a shirt or su'thin' out of the winder," Lockjaw went on reflectively.

"Are they good men, Charlie?" Doc Grimson asked quickly.

"Two of 'em are. Who're the other two, Lockjaw?"

"Big-Nose Adolph and Slim Jerry Coe."

"There ain't four better men loose," Charlie said.

"Then listen, boys," Doc said swiftly. "This gives us our chance. Most of those fellers are spread out in a semi-circle in front of us. If Charlie and Lockjaw's friends open up on 'em from behind they're goin' to get right flustered. We'll give 'em the signal, then we'll run for the barn, get our horses and come bustin' out on 'em."

LANCE STARED. "You mean run away?" he asked, unreasonably downcast.

"Hell, no!" Doc snapped. "We start at one end of that semi-circle and ride clear to the other. They'll be already flustered at being taken in the rear and charging them from the flank that way is goin' to bother 'em worse. Hell, boys, we'll roll 'em up like a carpet!"

Lance snatched off his shirt. "Mine's red," he yelled. "Nobody'll think we're runnin' up another white flag." He began to tie the shirt on the muzzle of his rifle.

Lockjaw was sent to the barn to tell Flint and to saddle himself a horse.

The red shirt had not been waved more than three times across the window before there was a sudden burst of firing from the hill. What Doc had foreseen came to pass. The attackers in front were thrown into disorder. Their backs were uncovered—and the men on the ridge top knew now to shoot!

Before they had really recovered from the half-panic into which they were thrown, six riders erupted wildly from the barn. They charged straight for the end of the semi-circle, six-guns blazing, swung sharply there and began to charge up the line.

That was a fight! Under the menace of the charging hoofs men stood up from cover all along the hillside, rifles and six-guns throwing lead. But it was impossible to withstand the fierceness of that attack. The fact that the men stood up localized the battle, made it difficult for those behind them to shoot effectively. And even from the hurricane decks of those racing broncs, the marksmanship of the outlaws was deadly.

They rode six abreast, separated by only a few yards. Charlie Parr, his white mustache whipping in the wind, his vivid blue eyes snapping fire; Doc Grimson, dark-clad, silent, his thumbs on the hammers of his twin .45s singing their death song; Lance, yelling like an Indian, his curly, reddish hair bare and snapping in the breeze; Flint, melancholy gone from him, features alive with the lust of battle; Lockjaw, wooden-faced, his six-gun the most destructive of them all; Hewitt, gray-haired, grim-faced, jaw set like a rock. There weren't a dozen men alive who could have stood up to them.

The first break in the formation came when Flint's horse went down. Lance pulled up and offered a stirrup. Together, Flint running at the horse's side, they formed a sort of cleaning up party, taking on the men who had escaped the others. It was hot work.

Ahead, Levitt, the stocky foreman of Lowery's spread, stood up, his Winchester barking rapidly. As Doc Grimson bore down on him the rifle clicked, empty. The foreman dropped it with a curse and flashed his Colt. Leaning on his horse's neck Doc shot it out of his hand. Levitt stood stunned. He had only time to ask himself whether such a shot represented marksmanship or accident before the Doc was on top of him, the six-gun raised. "May need you as a witness," he explained, eyes grimly humorous. Then the gun-barrel fell, and for Levitt the daylight went out.

Lowery, hiding behind a nearby mesquite bush, stood up as the four passed and fired several ineffective shots at them. Lance, coming behind, rode straight for him. The big ranchman's guns blazed once more and Lance's horse went down. Flint, thrown off balance, fell too. Lance rolled, came up and shot from his knees, just as Lowery's gun covered him for a finishing shot. The big man staggered, dropped his gun, fell forward on his face. Lance did not fire again. He knew that that shot had gone straight through the heart.

Along the line men were running. Several of them were shot down, for that fire from the top continued to be deadly. Others put up their hands, and they lived. Except for a few scattering shots from men who were too excited to realize what was happening, the fight was over....

CHAPTER 18
FRESH TRAILS

FOREMAN LEVITT came to life to find himself in the living room of the Flying M Bar ranch-house. Around him were grouped six men he had helped to frame and tried to kill. Behind them were others, members of his own and Ogalally's gang, who had escaped the guns of that final charge. Behind them were four hard-looking men, well-heeled with six-guns. Levitt's head ached badly. He shook it tentatively and groaned.

Hewitt looked down at him with his eyes hard. "Here's a glass of whisky, Levitt," he said. "We want to hear you do some talking. Better get ready for it."

Levitt drank and began to feel a little better. "I got nothing to say," he answered sullenly.

A large man, whom he dimly recognized as the first to escape of the original prisoners, moved in front of him, holding a Mexican by the scruff of the neck.

"This is Baby," the large man grinned amiably. "He's got plenty to say."

The Mexican whom Levitt recognized, and who also recognized Levitt, had plenty to say. He babbled brokenly, but Levitt understood him, and sufficiently to realize that Levitt's game was up. Levitt shuddered. If the Mexican's story ever got to court....

When Bautista had done, a slender man with icy eyes appeared before the foreman.

"Lowery's dead," he said quietly. "You're not—yet. Better talk, Levitt." Levitt recognized him, too; and the pupils of his eyes widened with fear. He knew Doe Grimson by reputation, but what Levitt chiefly thought of was his Colt being shot out of his hand and those grim words: "We may need you as a witness" before Doc's gun-barrel crashed down on his head. He gulped, his fingers twitching at his sides... and decided to talk.

"Talk on paper," Doc suggested. And Levitt did.

One of the men in the room was Ogalally Pete. "What're you going to do with us, Doc?" he asked. A good deal of his swagger gone.

"Why, Ogalally," Doc said pleasantly, "our business dealings have always been quite agreeable. In fact, so far, the advantage has been on our side. I reckon we won't hold a little fight against you. As far as I'm concerned, you're free to ride."

"That's what I call a white man!" Ogalally said, some of the swagger returning. "Come on, boys—let's ride!"

"Just a minute!" Hewitt's voice was deadly. "You and me got a little score to settle, Ogalally."

Doc Grimson looked chagrined and concerned at once. "Sorry, Hewitt," he apologized. "I forgot."

He had not forgotten. He had only hoped to get Ogalally

out before Hewitt forced this play. He guessed that Hewitt was no match for the outlaw in a gun-fight.

Ogalally's eyes narrowed "What's that about?" he asked.

"You killed my son—or you had him killed. You're answering to me for it—right now, you murderin' snake!"

Lance looked at Claire, saw the pallor of her face. "Just a minute," he interposed. "The shootin' was our fault. If anybody's going to take it up, it's got to be one of us. You and me will settle it, Ogalally."

"Oh, please," Claire pleaded. "My brother is dead. Another death won't bring Bill back."

Lockjaw looked surprised. "Why, he ain't dead, ma'am," he said. "Didn't I tell you about that? The boys met up with an old desert rat who come on your brother after Ogalally and them left him, thinkin' he was dyin'. The desert rat took care of him an' he's getting along fine. The boys there will tell you about it."

That broke the tension.

Charlie Parr clapped his hand to his forehead. "That Lockjaw," he groaned. "Get him out of my sight, boys, before I forget and shoot him. You got to excuse him for not speakin' up before, miss. He ain't right bright, 'count of his maw dropped him on his head when he was a weaner. She done forgot."

Ogalally and his bunch moved out and with them a few of Lowery's men, dazed at being let off.

ONE OF the four stiff-faced men put out a hand to Charlie Parr. "Looks like you wouldn't be needin' us any more, Charlie," he said, "We'll be gettin' along." He was stolid-looking, with an enormous nose.

Charlie shook hands with him and then with the other three. "Lockjaw tells me he knows where you're hangin' out," he said. "We may drop in and see you before long. We're shore plumb obliged to you boys."

"Hell, Charlie," the big-nosed man said. "We owed you all of that and then some."

Levitt tried to go too, but Flint Maddox's hard hand stopped him. He learned that he'd have to testify in court and take his chances.

"Not that we'll have the pleasure of listening to you," Doc Grimson told him. "It'll be mostly to put Hewitt in the clear. We are kind of used to being—oh—misunderstood, so it don't make much difference to us whether the charges stand or not."

"They won't," Hewitt promised vigorously. "I'll see to that."

Lance and Claire had been talking together in the corner—now they went outside. Doc Grimson looked at Charlie Parr and raised his eyebrows. More woman trouble! Keeping Lance from getting married to every pretty girl who came along had gotten to be one of the major tasks of his and Charlie's lives.

At his nod Charlie strolled out to the door. "Well, Claire," he said innocently, "we're gettin' along now. It's shore been mighty nice to meet up with you."

Lance looked sulky. He didn't see any rush. He hadn't had a minute to talk to Claire alone. It occurred to him suddenly that perhaps he needn't go at all. Perhaps he could have plenty of time—all his life—to talk to Claire. He saw himself happily married, settled on Hewitt's ranch, helping to build it up. Then he saw, also, his friends riding down the trail without him. And that wasn't a picture he particularly liked. Torn, undecided, he turned on his heel and walked off to think.

Presently, Doc's voice said at his elbow, "We understand, Lance. We're sure sorry—but we understand. A man likes to settle down and have some peace in his life."

Lance said sullenly, resentfully: "Who said anything about wantin' peace."

"I guess we aren't much good to a man that wants to settle down," Doc went on regretfully, as though he hadn't heard. "The free life's mighty fine, but it's sure to bring a hombre into trouble. Why, right now, the rest of us are fixing to do something that's sure to cause some kind of stir."

"What's that?" Lance asked quickly.

"Why, we thought we'd maybe collect some of Lowery's cattle. He's dead and won't need 'em now."

"Dang it!" said Lance.

"But the best of it is the horses," Doc added carelessly. "Lowery had one of the finest remudas I ever saw. We kind of thought while we was at it, we'd take them along too."

Doc could see that the hook went home hard. Lance had a passion for good horseflesh. Doc put out his hand: "So long, old timer," he said. "And the best of luck to you!"

LANCE LOOKED at the hand a moment. Then he brushed by it.

"Where in hell you think you're goin' that I ain't goin'?" he snapped. Doc winked at Charlie Parr, who grinned back at him knowingly.

When they had collected their things and were mounted,

Claire cried: "Oh, why do you have to go?" She looked near to tears as she turned pleadingly toward them.

Hewitt said: "We'd sure be mighty proud to have any or all of you stay on." He looked at Lance as he spoke.

Lance turned to Claire and his eyes were wistful. Reluctantly he said: "I reckon we're the rovin' kind—thankin' you plenty just the same."

As they rode off, the others noticed that he looked back frequently to where the girl and her father stood watching them. But when they were out of sight he turned eagerly to Doc.

"Those horses, now, Doc…" he began.

Charlie Parr breathed a sigh of relief and winked at Flint. The five of them were together again!